# Murder, Mayhem and Mystery. A Collection of Short Stories

Kevin William Barry

Published by Kevin William Barry, 2020.

MURDER, MAYHEM AND MYSTERY. A COLLECTION OF SHORT STORIES

**First edition. March 31, 2020.**

Copyright © 2020 Kevin William Barry.

ISBN: 978-1393891307

Written by Kevin William Barry.

# A Letter to Oscar's Sister

## By Kevin William Barry

D ear Miss Gonzales,
    Although we have never met, I am sure you know who I am, just as I am sure the first thing you will want to do with this letter, is tear it into a million pieces and throw the bits into a fire. But I implore you, please read the few heartfelt words I have written here before consigning these pages to the flames.

Two years ago when I first met your brother Oscar, I was immediately enamoured by his charm, ready wit and generous nature. It is unnecessary of me to expound on his many and varied virtues and talents, you more than anyone else will be fully aware of what an extremely special person dear Oscar was. We became great friends he and I, and his death will haunt me until the day I die.

Oscar and I shared a passion for many things, but our greatest love was for surfing. He and I spent many hours together, out beyond the breakers, waiting for the perfect wave. We would sit astride our boards, chatting about everything and nothing, regaling each other with tall tales of our various exploits with women or on the sporting field. It was during one of these happy sessions that he told me about his wonderful sister Elvira.

On many of these occasions he also spoke about his life back in Madrid before he came to live here in Australia. Although he loved his new country, he still missed many things from his homeland. The most *important of these was undoubtedly being able to see your beautiful, smiling face. He adored you Elvira, of that I am certain.*

*Oscar may have told you that I work in the finance industry. He may have also told you that my work frequently has me travelling abroad. In the first instance, at least, he has been misinformed, ostensibly by me. The truth is I work for AATIO, the Australian Anti-Terrorism Intelligence Origination. No I am not a spy, the undercover operatives on our team are far more intelligent, capable and resourceful than I could ever be. But when our government detects a real and credible threat to our way of life, and when, because of international protocols or other considerations the threat cannot be dealt with through more orthodox channels, they sometimes call on me to effect a less legitimate solution. You see AATIO employ me as an assassin.*

*No doubt you have heard of the recent assassination of Malamud Ben Mustafa, the Pakistani operative and second in charge of that country's Al-Qa'ida. I was the person who put the bullet through his evil black heart. AATIO got involved when they gleaned some very credible intelligence that an Al-Qa'ida sleeper, living in Sydney, was preparing to launch an attack on the nuclear waste facility at Lucas Heights. Mustafa was that sleeper's contact back in Pakistan and his death meant the sleeper and his associates had no other recourse than to abandon their plans to blow up the Lucas Heights facility.*

*I was recruited by AATIO three years ago, directly after my time in the Australian Army, where I spent nearly eight years as a sniper with the SAS. Since joining AATIO I have received further training in many forms of martial arts as well as various forms of weapons operation. My speciality however is with a long range sniper rifle. I hold the army record for the highest score over 1000 metres at the 2013 Department of Defence competition and the second highest score over 1200 metres. All this I tell you only so you may better understand how the recent, tragic events came to pass.*

*Six days ago I returned from an assignment in Afghanistan. The details of that assignment are unimportant other than to say that my time in that country was extremely difficult and stressful. I was so happy to be home again on safe Australian soil.*

*I caught up with your brother and a few other friends a couple of days later, and remember thinking that Oscar seemed a little over excited and that he kept making strange, veiled comments about the upcoming weekend. When I questioned him about his actions, he simply smiled and told me he was just looking forward to the play on Saturday. As you are aware, Oscar recently joined an amateur dramatic society and they were about to commence their production of Arthur Miller's 'Death of a Salesman' that Saturday. Oscar had been given the lead role and you will be proud to hear he did a wonderful job. His rendition of Willy Loman was totally enthralling. I was spellbound during the entire performance, and completely amazed at how he could so easily hide his normally strong, Spanish accent and adopt the speech and mannerisms of an American from New England so perfectly. Despite his merely amateur status, he was a truly accomplished actor.*

*Sunday was my thirtieth birthday, a big event in anyone's life. I had arranged with Oscar and a few other friends to meet at the Sovereign Hotel on Sunday evening and was looking forward to the party immensely. But I never got there.*

*Around midday on Sunday I left my apartment to go to the gym, but as I was about to get into my car, two men, dressed in what appeared to be some sort of military attire, wearing balaclavas over their heads and carrying what looked to be a handgun and a large, vicious looking knife, crept up behind me and threw a black cloth bag over my head. One of the men jabbed his gun into my side and warned me that if I made a sound he would kill me. They dragged me to a waiting van, shoved me in the back, and bound my hands and feet so I couldn't escape. Then one of the men clambered into the back with me while the other climbed into the driver's seat and drove off rapidly. From the semi military attire and heavy middle eastern accents of my attackers, it seemed obvious to me that my abduction was somehow related to my recent time in Afghanistan.*

*As the van made its way through the back streets of Sydney, I lay quietly on the floor listening out for any indication of where my abductors might be taking me. But with my head covered by the bag, unable to see out and trussed up like a turkey, I was blind. Although I got the impression from our speed and the loud traffic noise we had at one stage driven along the highway, I had no real idea where we were headed.*

*After about half an hour, the van slowed and slewed around to the left. I could hear from the change in the noise from the tyres that we were now driving along a gravel road. The van stopped and one of my abductors got out. There was the unmistakable sound of a roller door being pulled up and then the van drove inside what I was later to learn was a large abandoned warehouse. The van stopped once again, its rear door flung open and I was dragged out. With my kidnappers holding my arms in a vice like grip, I was marched through the warehouse into a room at the rear of the building.*

*I was constantly looking for an opportunity to escape, but until that time none had presented itself. But when the two men had bound my arms, I had clenched my fists tightly and kept my wrists straight. In this way, when I relaxed my arms the ropes around my wrists loosened slightly. I knew that if I had the opportunity, I would be able to get my hands free. That opportunity came a few minutes later.*

*My captors led me through a doorway into a small room. They pushed me back onto a hard plastic chair and ripped the bag off my head. It took a few seconds for my eyes to adjust to the bright light glaring in my face, but when they did I could see I was being held in a rectangular space about 3 metres by five metres. It had two doors leading off it, the one we had just entered and a second directly opposite. The room contained only the chair I was sitting on, and an old, chrome legged and a timber topped table with a portable CD player on it. A single, unshaded light bulb hung from the ceiling, filling the tiny space with blinding light.*

My two captors stood before me menacingly, brandishing large evil looking knives. Both still wore balaclava masks over their faces.

"You are about to die infidel," the taller of the two thugs hissed in an accent I recognised as Pakistani. "How painful that death is, depends upon your answers to our questions. We know who you are Australian dog, and we know what you have done. Tell us the name of your contact in Pakistan and how you reach him, or you will soon be begging your false God to deliver you from unbearable suffering."

I told the man I had no idea what he was talking about. I was just an employee of Granite Financial services and didn't know anyone in Pakistan. But all the time I was speaking, I was working on my bindings behind my back, trying to get my hands free.

The smaller of the two men crossed over to the back wall of the room and picked up a pick handle which had been leaning against it. Then the first kidnapper reached over and pressed a button on the CD player. The room was suddenly filed with loud dance music. I knew what this meant. They had turned on the CD player so that my screams when they tortured me would be drowned out by the music. If I was going to survive, I had to make my move now. As the smaller man approached me I leant back and kicked out with my bound feet, both hitting him squarely in his right knee. He screamed in agony and fell to the floor. The second thug lunged, but he wasn't quick enough. I pulled against my bindings and my hands came free. My right fist shot out punching him in the throat, then I grabbed his knife hand and pressed my thumb into the back of his hand, twisting the blade away from me and towards his stomach. I thrust the blade into his gut and he went down, clutching at his stomach, his shirt front covered in a rapidly spreading pool of blood. I pulled the knife out and quickly slashed the rope around my ankles. I was free.

But then the door through which I had been dragged just moments before, flew open and a young woman strutted into the room. She was dressed in an Australian Army uniform, her shirt open to the waist, the skin between her breasts sparkling with glitter. She had her long blonde *hair tucked up into her army slouch hat and her face, which was quite attractive in a sluttish sort of way, was heavily made up with bright red lips and huge false eyelashes. On her feet she wore a pair of black high heels and her nails were long and painted with blood red polish.*

*Something was wrong, dreadfully wrong.*

*She froze in her tracks, took one look at the two men lying on the floor and the huge, blood soaked knife in my hand and screamed.*

*"Jesus Christ," she yelled, then turned and bolted back through the door she had entered just seconds before. As she flung the door open I could see the inside of the next room was decorated with coloured lights and a large, hand painted banner stretched across the far wall up near the ceiling. In the centre of the room was a long rectangular table with twenty or so chairs arranged around its perimeter. The table was laden with food and drinks and in the centre was a large round chocolate cake. I couldn't see what was written on the cake, but no doubt it was the same greeting as on the banner.*

*"Happy Birthday Alex."*

*Someone in the other room yelled "surprise", but by that time I was on my knees, trying desperately to staunch the blood pulsing from the horrendous wound I had inflicted on your poor dear brother. I was too late. Long before the paramedics arrived, Oscar had died form massive blood loss.*

*It was all a prank. All a stupid joke, meant to frighten me witless before the "Australian Army stripper", burst in and "saved the day" and then me and my friends would spend the afternoon and evening celebrating my thirtieth birthday. All a dumb joke, gone horribly wrong. One of my best friends, your poor dear brother, was now dead, and another had had his kneecap damaged beyond repair.*

*It was my fault Elvira. I should have told them about my past, should have warned them that I had been trained by the army in unarmed combat and was a dangerous man, a man they were better off staying away from. I should have told Oscar that knowing me could quite possibly get him killed. But how was I to know he and my other friends would pull such a prank, and that it would all go so terribly wrong?*

*Someone called the police. They came and arrested me, charged me with the murder of your brother and for the assault against my friend Tim who had been taken to hospital with a broken knee. They led me away in handcuffs, took away my belt and shoe laces and then threw me into a cell at the Parramatta Police Station. Later an official from ATTIO came and saw me. He told me there was nothing they could do, that the incident was nothing to do with my employment at AATIO. Not that I had asked them to do anything anyway.*

*The following morning my lawyer, Mr Albert Pinkerton arrived, and shortly after I was led into an interview room where I gave my statement. When that onerous task was completed, the cops charged me officially once again, this time revising the charge to manslaughter.*

*My lawyer then accompanied me back to my cell where we discussed my upcoming trial. When we were finished I asked Mr Pinkerton if he might stay for a few minutes while I recorded a letter to you on the small tape recorder he carried with him. The words you have just read are those which I dictated.*

*I know you can never forgive me Elvira, just as I can never forgive myself. Perhaps I have made things worse by explaining that your brother's death was a freak accident, rather than a malicious act on my part, but I need you to know I loved your brother as if he were my own, and if I could, I would gladly take his place in the grave and restore him to his loving sister.*

*Alex.*

*I am sure you will find the contents of the letter most disturbing and for that you have my deepest apologies together with my sincere commiserations on the tragic death of your brother. Although I never met Mr Gonzales, in my capacity as Mr Randall's counsel, I attended his funeral on the twenty sixth. You may find a little consolation in the knowledge that he was obviously a much admired and loved young man.*

*With regard to Mr Alex Randall, it is my duty to inform you that Mr Randall died by his own hand on the twenty sixth of this month. He was found hanged from the bars of his cell, by a strip of cloth he had torn from his prison uniform. His last will and testament bequeaths his entire estate to you. I imagine it will be a few months before his estate is finalised but you should receive a cheque by the end of September.*

*If I can be of further assistance in this matter, please do not hesitate to contact me.*

*Yours sincerely*

*Albert J Pinkerton*

*Attorney at Law*

## The End

# Reginald Osborne is Blue

*A short story*
*by Kevin William Barry*

If one were to pose the question to those who knew him, what was Reginald Osborne like? The most commonly elicited response would be 'He was okay.... I guess'. If pressured, some may have added adjectives such as insular, or loner, or reclusive or even weird. The unkind may have even described him as creepy or cold.

But Reginald Osborne, thirty three years old, divorced and until recently, working as a claim's assessor with a medium sized insurance company, wasn't always that way. A decade ago he had been considered quite sociable, perhaps not exactly charismatic, but certainly engaging, and when amongst his own small circle of friends, often quite witty. Although Reginald could never have been described as particularly handsome, he was still quite attractive. He was of average height, or perhaps a little less, he had thick, wavy, dark hair which occasionally proved unruly if it got too long, pleasant though unremarkable features, and a passably athletic physique. He was kind and quietly spoken and always respectful of others.

Ten years ago he met Ester Smythe. She was a mousey little woman, quite petite, with pale ginger hair and equally pale blue eyes. She had a pleasant enough face, though in a certain light her nose looked decidedly beaky, and her ears stuck out just a little bit too much to be considered perfect. She was fourteen months Reginald's junior and their attraction for each other was instantaneous and undeniable. They fell in love and from that moment on, they were seldom seen apart. For those who moved within their enclave, their marriage eleven months later, seemed predestined, almost inevitable.

Just a few short months after their nuptials, Ester informed Reginald that she was pregnant, and seven months after that, following a long and extremely painful labour, Ester presented her husband with a son. He was a healthy, happy baby boy and no parents in the history of mankind ever loved a child more. They named him Nathan after Ester's paternal Grandfather.

For the next four years Reginald, Ester and Nathan lived a happy, relatively carefree life together. There were of course, those rare occasions which occur in every family, where things went a bit pear shaped, or unexpected expenses put a strain on their budget. But generally speaking they were content with their lot and greeted each new day with optimism.

Then a drunk driver lost control of his vehicle, veered off the road, jumped the kerb and crashed through the wall of the local kindergarten. Four year old Nathan was enjoying a nap on the floor on one of the foam mats the centre kept for that purpose. The Ford's front left hand wheel crushed young Nathan's chest as it passed over him. He never woke up.

The man who killed, or maybe we should say murdered, little Nathan Osborne, was called Damien Exeter. He was a forty two year old, unemployed factory worker, yet to acknowledge that he was an alcoholic. At the time of his arrest, his blood alcohol reading was just a smidgen under five times over the legal limit, prompting the arresting officer to comment "I'm surprised the bastard could even walk, let alone drive." No one pointed out the fact he obviously couldn't.

Originally Exeter was charged with manslaughter. But after a considerable amount of negotiating and plea bargaining by his defence lawyer, that charge was downgraded to culpable use of a motor vehicle causing death. He was tried and convicted and sentenced to nine years in prison. With good behaviour he would be out in six.

The day that Nathan died, something died in Reginald too. It also heralded the demise of Reginald and Ester's marriage. Some couples may have found a scintilla of solace in their love for each other, but for Reginald and Ester, this was not the case. Their grief simply fed off one another. Every moment they spent together was a reminder of the terrible loss they'd had to endure and eventually those constant reminders became too much to bear. When Ester asked for a divorce, Reginald simply nodded his head sadly, packed a few meagre, but essential belongings into a suitcase, and left.

He found himself a room in a cheap hotel close to his place of employment. It was sparsely furnished with just a single bed, an old, tattered armchair and a chest of drawers to store his clothes. There was a communal bathroom at the end of the hall and a resident's kitchen on the ground floor. It was an undeniably Spartan existence, but for Reginald at least, it was enough. Over the next six years Osborne rarely left his room, choosing instead to wait until Exeter's incarceration came to an end. He was counting down the days until the monster who had taken away his beautiful son and ruined his life was back out on the street where he could reach him.

Over the ensuing years, every semblance of the once sociable, cheerful man he had once been deserted him. He became a mere shell of his former self, fixating on the future and planning for the day Exeter was set free.

By some miracle Reginald was able to hold onto his job. Sometimes, in the beginning, one of his work colleagues might foolishly try to engage him in conversation. But if the subject wasn't work related Reginald would often look confused or simply ignore them. Eventually everyone just left him to his own devices. He buried himself in his work, arriving promptly at eight thirty every work day morning, working tirelessly throughout the day, and then leaving for his pathetic hotel room, just after five. As far as his employer was concerned, Osborne was the perfect employee. Sure he might be a bit strange, but no one could fault his work ethic.

But now the fateful day of Damien Exeter's release was at hand and for the first time in six years Reginald Osborne failed to show up for work. He had driven out to the prison on the outskirts of the city and now lay in wait for his quarry. Exeter was due to be released at one pm and Reginald and the razor sharp butcher's knife he carried with him would be there to greet him.

Dead on one o'clock the prison gates swung open. The man who strode through them, free as a bird, was instantly recognisable as Exeter. Sure he had shaved off the beard he'd once worn and he'd lost a considerable amount of weight over the past six years, but there was no doubt in Reginald's mind that this was the man he'd been waiting for, for so long.

As Exeter crossed to the bus stop on the other side of the road, Reginald calmly walked up to him. Before his victim could react Reginald drew the viciously sharp knife from behind his back and plunged it into Exeter's chest. The man looked stunned and took a step backwards in surprise. Reginald struck again and this time Exeter fell to the ground. Reginald knelt over him and once again plunged the knife into his victim's black heart. Again and again Reginald stabbed and stabbed in a frenzied, relentless attack which continued unabated until two prison guards raced across the road and dragged him off. They were too late. Exeter was already dead. One of the guards wrestled the knife from Reginald's blood soaked hand, twisted his arm painfully up behind his back to subdue him and slapped on a pair of handcuffs. Then he had Reginald lie face down on the ground while his colleague called the cops.

Now Reginald Osborne is sitting in interview room number three, inside the precincts of the Central City police station. The room is stuffy and overly warm. The air inside is rank with the odorous fug of too many unwashed bodies and the stench of cigarette ash. The floor is tiled with large, dirty, ceramic tiles, the walls painted in a colour best described as 'used to be white' and there is a bank of recessed florescent light tubes, blazing down brightly from the ceiling, onto a gun metal grey, Formica topped table. Around this table sits Reginald Osborne, next to him, his defence lawyer, Albert Pinkerton and opposite them the tall, dark and handsome personage of Detective Inspector Andrew Daniels and his sultry sidekick DC Jayne Usher. All have been in the room for over two hours and so far Reginald has only spoken once. Despite DI Daniels considerable skills and experience in interrogation procedures, that doesn't look likely to change.

"I need to get some coffee," Andrew states, shaking his head in exasperation and making his way to the door. "Anybody else want one. Everyone except Reginald answers in the negative. Osborne continues to play the mute.

"How's it going in there?" Andrew's boss, Superintendent Peter Miles, asks in the hallway outside the interview room.

The DI shakes his head. "So far he's only opened his mouth once. He simply said 'Exeter had to die."

"Who's Exeter?"

"The drunk who killed Osborne's son with his car six years ago."

"But wasn't the victim called Simpkins?"

"Yea. Exeter was released from prison yesterday. I think Osborne's killed the wrong man."

### THE END

# Lide's Luck

a short Story
by Kevin William Barry

Uncut diamonds. They're the perfect swag. They're small, light, high in value and, because they can be cut, they're almost impossible to trace. You can, for example, stuff a fortune of uncut, stolen diamonds in your pocket, and only your tailor will notice the bulge. Plus, if you're a registered gem cutter like Macalister Lide, your stolen fortune won't necessarily be eroded substantially by having to dispose of the uncut diamonds through someone who deals in stolen property.

Macalister Lide just loved diamonds. Marilyn Monroe believed them to be a girl's best friend, but her adoration of those sparkly crystals of highly compressed carbon paled into insignificance when compared to the passion Macalister Lide felt for them. He was particularly enamoured with those diamonds which belonged to someone else. Someone like 'Lindsay and Sons Jewellers.'

Macalister was fifty eight years of age. He was a small and wiry man, with a stooped posture thanks to too many years hunched over a workbench and with fading eyesight after spending those same years with a jeweller's loupe stuck, almost permanently, in his right eye. His complexion was a pale and unhealthy grey, like cigarette ash, and he exuded an aura of morose despair. Those who knew him attributed that despair, to a life filled with precious little love; or even companionship, poor diet and a distinct lack of exercise.

'Lindsay and Sons Jewellers', had been in existence for over one hundred years. Its founder, Edmund Lindsay, his sons, and for that matter even his grandsons, had died out years ago. Now the business was owned by a conglomerate of multinational business men and women, all of whom felt more than comfortable investing in the well established economic reliability of precious gems.

In a world infested with fashionable commodities like 'Bit Coins, the globe trotting socialites who now owned LSJ, knew that even though 'Bit Coins' were worth a fortune at the moment, only a fool imagined the make believe currency could maintain its stratospheric value indefinitely. Diamonds, rubies, emeralds and sapphires have been coveted since the dawn of mankind, and everyone at LSJ felt more than confident that would continue.

The 'Jewellers' bit of Lindsay and Sons Jewellers, could probably have been dispensed with in 2018. Sure the company still produced a small range of prestige jewellery for the discerning buyer, but the manufacture of such items was more out of respect for tradition than any sensible business decision. Today the real money was in the procurement of rare gem stones, the cutting and polishing of them, and then the on-selling of those sparkling jewels to the smaller, family owned companies which specialised in pandering to the whims of those who hankered for a bit of upmarket bling.

Macalister Lide had worked for LSJ for almost forty years, and considered himself a valuable employee. Sometimes, when he was enjoying one of his numerous cigarette breaks in the alleyway behind the old 'Lindsay and Sons', red brick warehouse and shop front; situated in one of the more affluent inner city suburbs; Macalister felt an surge of resentment for his employers.

"I do all the work," he complained to himself. "It's my skill and my experience which produce the beautiful gemstones those lazy bastards sell. I work my fingers to the bone so they can enjoy huge fortunes. Meanwhile I have to survive, almost penniless, on the pittance they pay me."

At which point, more often than not, Macalister Lide would hock up a big glob of tobacco blackened phlegm and, with practised ease, propel it across the lane way, splatting it against the side of one of the multitude of garbage bins scattered along the opposite wall. He was a heavy smoker. Forty plus, high tar coffin nails, filled his lungs each and every day. A chain smoker of the highest magnitude, he was seldom to be seen without a smoke in his mouth and like most tobacco addicts, Macalister constantly voiced the mantra, "I could give up if I wanted to, I just don't want to." He didn't fool anyone, least of all himself.

The resentment Macalister felt towards his employers had been growing inexorably now for almost a decade. Each day he racked his brain, searching for a way to steal some of the more valuable stock from Lindsay and Sons Jewellers, but such a task was not easily achieved. A great number of checks and balances had been put into place to make it nearly impossible for even the most tiny gems to be taken outside the premises without somebody noticing.

Before each piece was locked away in the large, walk in vault in the north east corner of the Lindsay and Son's facility, every gem stone was weighed, photographed and checked for authenticity, clarity, flaws, lustre, value etc by the chief valuer, then logged, both manually in a huge, leather bound ledger, and digitally on LSJ's mainframe. This happened every time a piece was taken in or out of the vault.

Plus, each time a gem left the strong room for processing, it had to be signed out by the employee who was to to perform the necessary work and checked back in again by the end of the day. Of course, the uninitiated might mistakenly assume that perhaps the tiny slivers and chips of gemstone removed during the cutting and faceting process might 'accidentally' make their way into someone's pocket. But even this was not the case. Gemstones are cut by fracturing, not abrading as one might do with a piece of metal. That means there is no 'saw dust' as such, only chips and slivers. So the weight of those chips and slivers, together with the finished gem, will always add up, almost exactly, to the weight of the original stone. If it doesn't, then questions are asked.

Besides, Macalister knew full well that even if such subterfuge was possible, the tiny bits had such meagre commercial value, it would take years if not decades, for him to collect enough to be considered worthwhile.

But now Macalister Lide had come up with a cunning plan.

On Monday, he had handed in his notice, telling his bosses he intended to leave the employ of Lindsay and Son's Jewellers in a month's time. He explained to them that rather than waiting to reach the normal retirement age of sixty five, he was going to retire early. But of course, there was an ulterior motive for his resignation.

Six days later, very late on Sunday evening, Macalister was ready to put his plan into effect. In the alleyway behind the LSJ building there were two strategically placed CCTV cameras. The cameras were never monitored, but rather simply recorded the comings and goings which might occur in the alleyway. Sunday night at eleven forty seven, the lane way was in almost total darkness. Only a single street lamp near the entrance to the alley, provided any illumination. Macalister, wearing latex gloves and dressed all in black, pulled his balaclava down over his face and, without looking up at the cameras, directed a jet of black aerosol spray paint over first one and then the other CCTV cameras, coating the lenses with an impenetrable coating of black enamel. He then retrieved the equipment he'd left in a large, black bag at the entrance to the alleyway and made his way to the roller door at the rear of the LSJ building.

The roller door could be opened from the inside by simply pressing a button. But from the outside, it could only be raised by operating a remote control device. This remote control was, at all times, kept in the possession of the chief valuer. He even took it home with him on weekends. But Macalister knew the roller door mechanism also had an 'electronic eye' sensor, inside the building, a metre or so back from the door and a similar height from the floor. This 'electronic eye' was supposed to prevent the door accidentally closing on a vehicle while it was exiting the warehouse.

Macalister dove into his bag and extracted a thin, flat sheet of stiff blue plastic. The sheet, was rectangular in shape, one metre wide by one point five metres long. It was also attached, along the shorter edge, to a two metre long length of thick fencing wire. Macalister pushed the plastic sheet into the narrow gap between the bottom of the roller door and the concrete floor of the building, straightening the coiled up fencing wire as he went. When he felt he had reached the point directly below the 'electronic eye', he bent the remaining wire at a right angle and then twisted it anti-clockwise ninety degrees. The sheet of plastic stood upright, standing on its edge, breaking the beam from the 'electronic eye' and the roller door's motor slowly began to raise the door.

Before the door rose half a metre Macalister lay on his back and quickly rolled under it. He reached back outside, retrieved his bag, sprang to his feet and then hurried across the warehouse to the keypad for the burglar alarm system. He knew he had no more than thirty seconds to enter the correct code to deactivate the alarm. Using the battery drill he'd brought from home he quickly drilled two small holes, approximately thirty millimetres apart, through the plastic face plate, up near the top of the keypad. Into these holes he'd pushed two pieces of stiff copper wire. Working quickly he attached the high amperage cables from a small portable arc welder; also brought from his home; to the wires. He plugged the welder into a nearby power outlet and threw the switch. There was a flash of light from the keypad and a cloud of acrid black smoke billowed from the box. The high amperage DC current from the welder had fried the delicate electronics of the alarm system, rendering it inoperable.

Macalister hurried back to the roller door and closed it. With the door closed and the alarm disabled, he felt the chance of discovery was very slim indeed. Now he could take his time opening the vault. He smiled to himself. So far everything was going to plan perfectly.

He made his way quickly across the warehouse floor to the north east corner of the building. As he ran he reached into his top pocket and pulled out his cigarettes. He flicked the pack open, selected a fag and lit up. Immediately he was overcome by an irrepressible coughing fit. He dropped his bag and bent over at the waist, his whole body shaking uncontrollably until the fit subsided and he was once again able to catch his breath.

"Shit!" he swore to himself. "I gotta give these things up. They'll be the death of me one day." Of course, Macalister had made that particular promise to himself on numerous occasions over the years, and even as he said it once again, he knew in his heart, his words were hollow. They were meaningless guff. He was heavily addicted. He was a smoker and would be until the day he died.

Ironically, the building which now housed 'Lindsay and Sons Jewellers' had, until a few years ago, been a cigarette distribution centre. The warehouse belonged to one of the partners who owned LSJ, and when the tobacco industry went into free fall, it had been decided to close the distribution centre and relocate Lindsay and Son's Jewellers into the now empty warehouse. The building was, of course, far to big for the company's needs. But it had a small street front showroom, an excellent burglar alarm system and a large walk in strongroom. Plus, the gemstone business was more than profitable enough to compensate for the wasted floor space in the main warehouse. Now, inside the warehouse, there was row upon row of empty pallet racking, a thick coating of dust, a few miles of cobweb and precious little else.

The vault itself was four metres square, with a two point two metre high ceiling. The walls and ceiling were six hundred millimetres thick concrete, reinforced with twelve millimetre steel mesh. The floor was also reinforced, not just the floor directly under the vault itself, but also an area three metres all around. This was to prevent any ingress into the strongroom by a determined thief with a jackhammer bent on tunnelling his way in. The door to the vault was heavily fabricated steel, also six hundred millimetres thick, with internal hinges unable to be accessed from the outside. Six, one hundred and fifty millimetre diameter, tungsten steel bolts protruded into the right hand door frame when the vault was locked. In the centre of the door, an electronic keypad controlled the locks and the hydraulic actuator which opened and closed the massive door.

Macalister stubbed out his cigarette, making sure the butt was placed securely in the small glass jar he'd brought specifically for that purpose. The last thing he wanted to do was leave behind something which would lead the cops straight to him. He placed his bag on the floor next to the strongroom door and addressed the vault's keypad almost reverently. There would be no drilling holes and frying the delicate electronic circuitry this time. Macalister wanted the door open, not permanently shut. From his bag of tricks he selected a small jar of black powder and a soft bristled brush. The pot contained a few grams of fingerprint powder which he'd made by mixing talcum powder with crushed charcoal. He gently applied the powder to the keypad with the brush. Six of the numbered keys had fingerprints on them, so he knew those six numbers made up the code which would open the vault. But in what sequence did those six keys need to be pressed?

Macalister smiled to himself and removed a sheet of paper from his top pocket. On it were printed the birth dates of all the LSJ's owners, plus the dates of their spouse's and children's birthdays. Over the past couple of years Macalister had made note of those dates as each of the partner's birthdays came around. He'd also been able to glean the rest of their family's information by accessing their 'social media' pages. Plus the list contained the dates of wedding anniversaries, important dates from within the history of the company, plus a list of the most commonly used, six digit PIN numbers, according to the indispensable computer search engine Macalister used.

Checking the numbers quickly, he worked his way down the list, crossing out all those which didn't fit the required criteria. Surprisingly he had just seven numbers left when he reached the bottom.

But he wondered if even that small number was too many. If he entered the wrong PIN on his cell phone, he knew he had just three more attempts to get it right. If he didn't, the phone would lock up and he'd have to contact the service provider to get it unlocked. Was the keypad on the strongroom similarly protected? He shrugged. He knew he'd reached the point of no return in his escapade. Either he would be successful today, or he would fail in his attempt. Giving up now could only result in one outcome, failure. Slowly he began to enter the first of the seven codes. On the third number the keypad lit up, there was a loud clunk followed by a quiet whirring sound as the vault's six, huge, cylindrical bolts wound back into the door. Seconds later the hydraulic rams which actuated the opening and closing of the massive vault powered up and the door swung open. Macalister chuckled to himself. He'd done it. Now all he had to do was fill his bag with the most valuable gems and make his escape.

Now the more astute readers of this transcript will have already seen a fatal flaw in Macalister's cunning plan. Come Monday morning, when the premises were opened for another day of trading at eight thirty, the robbery would undoubtedly be discovered. Any investigator worthy of the title would immediately suspect it had been an inside job. With only five people working for Lindsay and Sons Jewellers at the time, Macalister would automatically be under suspicion. It also followed that, supposing the detective assigned to the case wasn't a complete novice, evidence would be eventually be found and Macalister would be deemed culpable.

Allow me then to belatedly introduce Ignatius Malloy.

Ignatius Malloy was twenty seven years old. He was tall and lean, heavily tattooed, and wore his dark, greasy hair unfashionably long. Although not overly bright, Ignatius was more than adequately equipped mentally, to clear away coffee cups, empty waste paper bins, clean the staff lunch room and toilets, mop the floor in the showroom and polish the display case glass to a crystal clear lustre. Ignatius had been employed by LSJ as a cleaner. Or at least he used to be. He'd lasted a total of just four days before the results of a security check instigated at the time of his interview came back showing he'd recently been in the slammer for not so grand larceny. Of course, he'd been sacked on the spot. The details of his crime wouldn't exactly warrant a mention in a book called 'The Worlds Most Notorious Robberies.' After all, he had only been nabbed for shoplifting. But a business dealing in millions of dollars of precious gems, couldn't be too careful, so Ignatius was given his marching orders. It is fair to say that a criminal record, together with a recent sacking, would probably elevate Ignatius Malloy to the top of any list of suspects. But as with all good scenarios, there was also another misleading factor to be added to the mix. Ignatius Malloy was a Canadian / Australian dual citizen. He'd emigrated to 'The land down under' when he was just nineteen, and now, having realised getting a job in Oz was going to be as likely as going a whole day on social media without some scantly clad bimbo asking him to like their 'Awesome' page, Ignatius had decided to return to the land of his birth. In fact, he'd told Macalister he was due to fly out early Monday morning. Just two hours before the commencement of trade at LSJ.

In addition, Macalister had already instigated contingencies to avert suspicion from himself. He would turn up, ready for work Monday morning, just as he had done almost every Monday morning for the past thirty eight years. Macalister was certain such actions would throw the cops off his trail. Surely whoever had stolen the gemstones would be on the run? Ignatius Malloy certainly was!

Then, in three weeks time, when he was due to take early retirement, Macalister would bid his former employers a fond farewell and piss off to Phuket. There he intended to live in luxury for the rest of his life.

Macalister smiled to himself once again as he strode confidently into the strongroom. There on the shelves in front of him was over three million dollars worth of precious gems. There was also a considerable amount of cash. That was something else Macalister had gleaned over the years, knowledge of all the retail companies who preferred to deal off the records. Of course, there could only be one reason why a company would rather swap a briefcase full of dollars for precious stones than use a bank transfer, and that was because they were trying to hide the transaction from someone. Normally that someone was going to be either the cops or the taxman. Soon those names would prove nearly as valuable to Macalister as the gems themselves.

"Okay!" he said to himself. "First things first."

Once again he dove into his black bag. He pulled out a tiny paper envelope and extracted a long dark hair. He had collected the hair a few days previously, from a comb he'd found in Ignatius Malloy's locker. Carefully he'd placed the hair on the edge of one of the felt covered display trays, containing a king's ransom of rubies. Undoubtedly the planted evidence would be found by the cops and the hair's DNA would lead them directly to Ignatius. Of course, Macalister knew there was a slight chance he might leave some of his own DNA behind. But as he'd handled the company's gemstones almost daily, it was always possible such DNA was there innocently, inadvertently carried into the vault by the chief valuer when he'd returned the jewels Macalister had been working on at the end of the day. At least that would be what Macalister would offer as a reason. On the other hand, there could be no, non criminal, justification for Ignatius Malloy's DNA being anywhere near the vault, let alone inside it.

Macalister opened the top of his bag, unzipped the separate internal compartment, selected the most valuable diamonds from the shelves, and began to empty the trays of precious stones into it. After a few moments he paused, once again for one of his dreaded coffin nails. He tapped one out of the pack, lit the end with a disposable lighter and took a huge drag. This time the smoke didn't catch in the back of his throat. Smiling to himself at how clever he'd been, he nonchalantly blew the smoke into the air, accidentally blowing it straight into the sensor of the smoke alarm attached to the ceiling above the shelves. Suddenly the quiet night was shattered by a terrific clamour. The smoke alarm wasn't connected to the burglar alarm Macalister had disabled just a few minutes before, it had its own circuitry and was connected to a large klaxon. Half the city was able to hear the terrible din.

But there was worse to come. To protect the valuable contents of the vault, the fire alarm was also connected to the hydraulic ram which opened and closed the strongroom door. Macalister failed to hear the hydraulics power up over the noise of the alarm, and by the time he realised the door was closing, it was already too late too make his escape. He was trapped.

Macalister cursed his bad luck, cursed his stupidity, and cursed the day he'd ever taken up smoking. He was trapped, and there wasn't a hope in hell he would be able to unlock the vault from inside. He realised he was done for. He knew he would not be spending the rest of his life living it up in Phuket, but spending it in prison instead.

But that wasn't to be the case. As the fire alarm continued to alert everyone in the vicinity that something was amiss, the second fail-safe aspect of the system came in to play. Slowly the strongroom began to fill with Halon gas.

Halon gas is often used in fire prevention systems for enclosed areas, especially in cases where soaking everything in water might cause considerable damage. It's not flammable, nor does it support combustion. It works by displacing the air a fire needs to exist. Without air, a fire suffocates.

So did Macalister Lide.

# The End

# Abducted

*A short story by*
*Kevin William Barry*

My wife's been kidnapped. Her name is Felicity Bertoli. Yea, *that* Felicity Bertoli. She's been missing three days and the cops are clueless.

You might think being married to a movie star would be like a dream made in heaven, She is after all, incredibly beautiful, tall and statuesque with that long, lustrous, raven black hair, flawless golden skin and those almond shaped, deep blue eyes. But she's also rich and famous and one of those two things has led some greedy or sick bastard to snatch her from our home.

My money's on the famous aspect. Sure her fame is great for opening doors. You know you'll always get a table in a restaurant, even if it's the latest, most chic eatery on the planet and normal people have to wait months for an opening, and that's great. The fact we always get first class treatment, with people fawning over us like we're royalty (or rather Felicity is) wherever we go is nice too. But I know from previous experience Felicity's on screen presence can sometimes attract the wrong type of fan. I've lost count of the number of times we've received weird phone calls in the middle of the night. Or unpleasant, suggestive e-mails. Or had stuff jammed in the mailbox, highly inappropriate things like used condoms, left there by the sickos, the men whose warped and deranged minds have convinced them their lust for the beautiful woman on their TV or movie screens is true love. They seem to think those used condoms are some sort of proof of their undying devotion. Despite the increased police presence in our street at the moment, there was even one in the mail box this morning. The worst nut bags seem to be the Looneys who call her Colopo, the weird, yet strangely sexy alien she played in the blockbuster movie 'Alien Vermin'. Yea, we really know the dude's deranged when that happens.

The cops originally thought Felicity's kidnap might be about money, but now they're not so sure. I'll explain their reasoning. A week ago I was in Athens. I'm part of the Special Effects team working on the new movie 'Lethal Odyssey'. If one of the characters gets his or her leg blown off, I'm the guy who has to use bits of silicone, maybe some polyurethane foam, putty, liquid latex, make-up and lots of fake blood to make the injury look real. You could call me a specialist make-up consultant I suppose. In fact that's how Felicity and I met, on the set of 'Alien Vermin'. I'm the one who transformed her from a stunningly beautiful human actress into the sultry, silvery blue alien translator who captured the hearts of millions of movie goers.

But I digress. As I said, a week ago I was in Athens and had been for nearly three weeks. Felicity was back here. We'd spoken on the phone or by Skype every day, sometimes more than once a day, so I knew she was safe. At least she was until Sunday. That was the day I boarded a Jumbo to come back home. Seventy two hours later I pulled into our driveway and parked my Mercedes behind Felicity's Porsche. The front door was unlocked, which in itself was unusual, and the radio was on, turned up loud. I carried my bag into the foyer, calling Felicity's name to let her know I was home. But she was nowhere to be found.

At first, I wondered if she'd just gone out. Maybe her sister or one of her friends had popped around for a visit and they'd decided to go out shopping together. But I soon realised something was wrong. Our bedroom was a mess, one of the easy chairs next to the bed was tipped over, the mirror above Felicity's dressing table was smashed and there was a broken hair brush lying on the floor next to one of the walls. Above it was a mark on the wall at about head height, as if someone had thrown the brush against the wall. Or, as the investigating police officer, Detective Inspector Roger Dark surmised, the brush had hit the wall after missing the person Felicity had thrown it at.

Lying on the bed was Felicity's handbag. Her wallet, containing almost three thousand dollars in cash and all her credit cards was still inside. As were her car keys and phone. The fact the money hadn't been taken, nor any of her jewellery, lead me to believe her abductor had not been motivated by greed. DI Dark agrees.

Of course, there is another, less sinister explanation. My wife has simply gone off on her own to 'get her head straight'. She's done that sort of thing before, simply packed a bag and drove off down the coast to some remote, beachside hideaway without telling a living soul. Sometimes she just needs go somewhere quiet; to lie in the sun and contemplate whatever it is that's messing with her head. Unfortunately, lots of things seem to mess with her head.

You see, as wonderful as it is to be married to the foremost movie actress in the country, it can also be a bit of a nightmare. The punters only get to see the ravishing, always loving, always happy, female character portrayed on the big screen. They don't get to endure the tantrums and the narcissism. The bullying and the ranting and raving at the people who are only doing their job. The drama queen tears when things don't go precisely as she wants them to, or the almost pathetic, barely credible portrayal of self doubt when things on set go a bit haywire.

Plus, she's thirty four now, and everyone in the industry knows that for some actresses, the two decades between thirty five and fifty five can be a defining period in their career. Too old to play the pretty young love interest, and too young for the more gritty, character driven roles like those given to Meryl and Dame Judith. For some actresses, thirty five can mean the end of their careers. They just never manage to re-establish a niche as an older character actor. The next twenty years are going to be make or break for Felicity. Already the formerly abundant prime offers are beginning to dry up, and just before I went to Europe, her manger, Paula Simpkins, started making noises about putting out some feelers for a new 'Older woman / Younger man Romcom' said to be in the pipeline. So I know she's worried. She's told me so. Constantly.

But there are a couple of things which lead me to believe she hasn't just gone off on a spur of the moment sabbatical. Firstly there's her car. She loves her little Porsche. But the damn thing attracts attention like flies to a honey jar. So she would have stuck it in the garage and had her sister or Paula arrange a nondescript rental. She would not have left it parked on the driveway. Secondly, as already stated, she didn't take her handbag or credit cards. Felicity Bertoli leaving the house without her fantastic plastic just doesn't bare contemplating. Thirdly, one of the first things I did when I got back from Athens was to check the safe in our bedroom. All her jewellery was still locked away safely, as was her tiny Smith and Wesson 638 revolver, plus her spare phone. Had she been able to, she would have taken those last two items with her no matter what. Especially the phone. She bought that after those tabloid journalists hacked into the British royal family's phones last year. It's a basic, prepaid unit, with long term credit, no camera and definitely no GPS. It's registered to a fictitious person and the only other two people who know its number are me and her sister. In other words, there's no way in hell anyone could track her down, but she'd still be able to get hold of someone in an emergency. And Felicity has a lot of emergencies.

She would have also taken the gun for protection. It's a tiny little thing, barely weighing half a kilo. But the damn thing takes a .38 calibre slug that can really pack a punch. Trust me I know. She shot me once in a fit of rage after I refused to back her up during an argument with the her sister. Luckily it was only a through and through flesh wound and we were able to convince the doctors at the A&E and the cops that it was an accident. Princess Felicity got some free publicity and I got a ride in an ambulance. Lucky me.

My point is she wouldn't have deliberately left the house without those things. At least I think she wouldn't have.

At 10:00 am Kimberley Clarke turned up for our daily update with me and DI Dark. Kimberley is Felicity's PR consultant and for the past three days she's been desperately and unsuccessfully trying to keep a lid on this thing. She's a petite blonde, quite cute in a 'Girl Next-Door' type way, twenty six years old with a five year old daughter and an ex husband who's only just now starting to realise he's been a complete knob letting her get away. She's a human dynamo, one of the most capable people on the planet and totally indispensable. Felicity treats her like she's a piece of dirt.

She greeted me with a chaste kiss and asked me how I was holding up, then we stood together, looking out the French windows, along the road at the bottom of my drive, as DI Dark's Ford wound its way up the hill, weaving through the throng of Paparazzi vultures who have been circling, desperately searching for a titbit of tabloid carrion to throw to their ravenous audience. They've been there twenty nine hours, ever since Felicity's kidnap became public.

As prearranged, when he reached the gate at the bottom of the drive he called me on my cell phone and I flicked the switch to the automatic gates and let him through. We'd disconnected the buzzer and intercom on the gate on the second day of the ordeal so I could occasionally get a second's respite from the insatiably inquisitive media scrum camped by the roadside. Two uniform cops now constantly patrolled the area to keep out the riff raff who refuse to respect my privacy.

Kimberley and I greeted Dark at the door and led him and his broody, silent partner through to the living room. To my unasked question he shook his head dolefully and took a seat. His sidekick stood with his back to the window and crossed his arm across his chest. He's a dark haired, squat and muscular man whose stance somehow reminded me of a Sumo wrestling match I'd once seen in Tokyo.

"Any progress?" Kimberley asked as she lowered herself onto the white, kid leather armchair next to mine.

Dark pulled out his note book and opened it to an appropriate page. "We questioned your housekeeper once again about Ms Bertoli's movements in the days prior to her disappearance," he told us. "She confirmed that your wife seemed concerned about something, but couldn't say what. She also went on to say Ms Bertoli frequently seemed worried about something or other and so she didn't really take much notice. As you told me, Mrs Lambert has Sundays and Mondays off, so the last time she saw your wife was Saturday afternoon around 4:30 thirty." He glanced at his notebook for further inspiration. "You spoke to her around 6:15 fifteen am Sunday, our time, from Athens just before you boarded your flight home. So as far as we can ascertain, she went missing sometime between then and your arrival here around 8:00 pm Monday. This is further substantiated by the CCTV footage we lifted from your security system. It shows Ms Bertoli laying out by the pool from 9:12 until 10:16 am on Sunday. She enters the house at 10:19 and doesn't reappear. Sometime between 10:19 Sunday and your arrival here at 20:07 Monday your wife disappeared."

Of course, everything DI Dark said was just rehashing old information. There was nothing new there at all.

"We still don't know how whoever snatched Felicity did it," Kimberley pointed out.

"Well according to the security consultant I had examine your system yesterday," Dark explained, once again consulting his notes. "There's a blind spot in your CCTV coverage of the estate." He gets up from the lounge and crosses to the French windows overlooking the swimming pool, indicating we should follow him.

"The blind spot is caused by that beach umbrella to be precise," he explains, pointing to one of our huge, hexagonal, blue and white striped shade umbrellas, next to one of the chaise lounges on the tiles a metre or so from the edge of our huge, kidney shaped pool. "It blocks the line of sight from the security camera fixed to the south east corner of the house. There's a blind spot, or rather strip, all the way from this door to the gate in the back fence. That must be the way Ms Bertoli's kidnapper came in and out."

I nodded to show him I understood, but his theory just didn't make sense. We'd had a security consultant of our own, a highly regarded expert in his field, design and install the system for us. There's simply no way he would have made such a amateurish mistake. And yet that's exactly what must have happened. How else could someone break into our house and abduct my wife without being seen?

"No suspects?" I asked.

DI Dark looked at me, considering his options before he finally broached the subject I'd expected he might bring up since the beginning. "How long have you been married?" he asks.

"Just under three years."

"Then you'll know that generally your wife is a much loved public figure...But she's also made quite a few enemies?"

"Yes," I answer. What else can I say?

"Well, we've spoken to a few characters over the past three days. People who are known to hold a grudge against Felicity. So far we haven't been able to make an arrest, but I'm certain it's just a matter of time."

For the next few hours we went through the list of names DI Dark had already compiled as possible suspects. I added a few more. Kimberley mentioned a couple of others. Dark had his work cut out for him.

Eventually he and his beefcake shadow took their leave and Kimberley and I were left alone to rack our brains some more, struggling our way through an unappetising late lunch as we did so. By three, we'd had enough, both of the over spiced rice dish

Mrs Lambert had prepared for us and of worrying about Felicity. I made us coffee and took it out onto the tiled patio surrounding the swimming pool. We sat side by side on the chaise lounge under the infamous shade umbrella, silently considering our next move.

Kimberley noticed it first. "The umbrella's been moved!"

"What?"

"The umbrella's been moved. Look, you can see a dark, circular stain on the tiles where it sat previously. It used to be over here."

She was right. It had been moved. Of even greater significance was the fact that, had it not been, the CCTV camera wouldn't have been obscured. Like Siamese twins joined at the brain Kimberley and I both came to the same conclusion about what that meant.

"Shit."

I raced off to the bedroom and grabbed Felicity's spare phone. I couldn't risk using mine or the land line just in case the media mongrels outside had hacked into them. I grabbed the phone book from Felicity's office, opened it to 'MOTELS' and began to dial.

"Hi can I speak to Jessica Wilkins?" I asked the receptionist when she answered.

"I'm sorry, Sir. We have no one here by that name. Are you sure you've got the right motel?"

I apologised, thanked her for her help and hung up. Not that one!

"Who's Jessica Wilkins?" Kimberley asked as I dialled the next motel on the list.

"Lead female role in the movie 'Innocent Until Proven Deadly,' I told her. "It was the first major movie Felicity ever did. I'll bet my last dollar that's the name she'll be using."

I was right. Though it took me seventeen phone calls to prove it.

"Miss Wilkins is not taking any phone calls at present Sir," the man on the other end of the line declared. "Can I take a message?"

I hung up. Nuh.

I scurried back into the bedroom to collect some bits and pieces, into the kitchen for the item I'd placed in the freezer that morning, then had Kimberley drive me to my office. It's in a nondescript, steel and corrugated iron warehouse over in the city's south side industrial park. The boys and girls on the team call it 'Hogwarts,' because that's where we do our Special Effects magic. The warehouse is full of all sorts of pyrotechnic gear, specialised movie props, CGI equipment, miniature sets and of course, all the goodies I use to change people's appearance. At the time, it also had a couple of cars parked in the back lot while the rest of the team were still working in Athens. Dave Stratford's old Toyota was there and his keys were in the top, left hand drawer of his desk. Two hours later, having swapped the plates for a bogus set from the props department, I'm behind the wheel of Dave's car, heading south along the coast road to the 'Paradise Motel.' My wife is in room 209.

It took me just over an hour to drive the eighty two kilometres to Felicity's motel. I parked the car across the street and made my way around the back to room 209. I checked my reflection in the window of 208 and then banged on Felicity's door. She opened almost immediately.

"Oh My God," she said, holding her hand up to her mouth and smiling in surprise. "Darling, is that you? What the hell are you doing here? How did you find me."

I ignored her, barged inside, slamming the door shut behind me. "Are you insane?" I hissed. "You falsified your own kidnap. Why? This is some stupid publicity stunt to get yourself back in the headlines, isn't it?"

Her smile told me my assumption was right. She'd set it all up just to get her name back in the limelight again. She nodded cheekily.

"Does Paula know about your stupid hair-brained scheme?"

"Of course not," she replied, trying to make light of the whole situation. "How'd you find me anyway? And what's with the disguise? Oh! I know, you clever man, it's just in case the media tried to follow you. You didn't want to let the cat out of the bag. Clever old you." Then she went on to tell me how smart she'd been, setting up her own fake kidnapping, giggling happily at how she was sure 'her ordeal' would create renewed interest in her flagging career, not even considering for a moment all the people who had spent the past three days searching for her, all the people who were worried sick that she might be in danger or already dead. Her sister hadn't slept a wink since she went missing. Her manager Paula was tearing her hair out trying to find out what had happened, not to mention the manpower wasted by the police and the concern she was causing her loyal fans. Stupid, selfish bitch.

But there was something she hadn't considered when formulating her ill-conceived plan. How her husband might react. I grabbed her by the shoulders and pushed her back onto the bed. For a second she looked angry that I had the audacity to manhandle her. Then the look of anger was momentarily replaced by a smile, perhaps she thought my actions were a prelude to some 'rough-house' foreplay. Perhaps she thought I wanted her on the bed because I was overcome by lust after being apart for nearly four weeks. She was wrong.

With my left hand I reached across the bed, grabbed a spare pillow and pressed it over her face. My right hand reached around behind my back, searching for the tiny Smith and Wesson 638 revolver tucked in the back of my belt. I whipped it out, pressed the barrel into the pillow directly above her face and squeezed the trigger. The pillow deadened the noise of the gun slightly, but still there was a sharp pop, and a handful of feathers were thrown into the air. Felicity shuddered and twitched for a few seconds and then lay still. I checked her pulse. She was dead.

I emptied the disgusting contents of the condom one of her adoring fans had left for her just that morning on the bedspread next to her, flushed the Durex down the loo and left. An hour and twenty minutes later I was back at my office.

Felicity had given me the perfect opportunity to do what I had been wanting to do for almost a year. Her timing had given me an iron clad alibi for the time of her kidnap, I was in Athens. The disguise I'd adopted was nothing to do with keeping clear of the paparazzi. You see I was certain there would be CCTV cameras around the motel, they're everywhere these days. Now when the cops discover her body and check the footage, they'll see an overweight, middle aged, balding man being admitted to her room just before seven. At one stage, as I was pretending to check my appearance in the reflection of the window next door, I lifted my left hand to straighten a wayward hair. Anyone looking would notice that the 'perps' left ring finger was missing; one of the easiest special effects to accomplish by the way. Mine isn't.

Finger prints, well I wore latex gloves the whole time and the only things I touched in the room were Felicity, the pillow, the door knob to the room and Felicity's little handgun. That guns now sitting at the bottom of the Salat river one hundred and twenty kilometres north of the city.

So what about the dreaded DNA? Well we're talking about a motel room, a veritable cesspool of DNA left behind by the multitude of guests who have resided there. To find a specific bit of DNA; that which came from the person who killed my poor wife, would be almost impossible. Except for that glob of semen I left for the cops to find that is. The sample came from the condom one of Felicity's fans left in our mail box this morning. I don't know who he was, but from the CCTV footage from the camera trained on the postbox, I can tell you he was an overweight, middle aged, balding man. I can also tell you that his left ring finger was missing.

Of course, I don't have such a perfect alibi for the time of Felicity's death as I did for her kidnapping, but should the need arise, I'm certain Kimberley will back me up if I tell the cops I was having dinner at her place until around midnight. Kimmy's great like that.

Have I told you what a wonderful woman she is?

### *The End*

# The Money Lender

A short story
by Kevin William Barry

The woman was morbidly obese. She heaved open the taxi's rear, passenger side door and oozed inside. She came in head first, crawling in over the vinyl bench seat on hands and knees, wriggling her 'Wide Load' arse through the gap between the centre door post and the back of the seat, and then rolled herself upright and planted her enormous buttocks on the seat. The taxi lurched and sunk downwards alarmingly under the duress of the massively increased load, and the interior filled with the choking stench of her body odour. Her stomach sat on her knees, her breasts lay on her stomach and her numerous chins squashed against her chest and collar bone like a scarf made of uncooked sausages.

She was dressed in something straight off the cover of 'Skydiver Weekly.' The loose and shapeless garment, if indeed one could call it a garment, was a muted pale salmon pink with darker pink, sweat stained patches under her arms, across her spreading stomach and under her sagging boobs. In the sweltering, tropical heat, her face was dripping with sweat and she was panting like a greyhound after a big win on the track.

"Where too?" the driver asked.

"Corner of Fifth and Vine please," she wheezed breathlessly.

"Fifth and Vine it is."

The driver checked his mirrors, made sure all the blind spots were vehicle free, flicked on the right indicator and pulled out into the traffic. He'd only been driving the cab, part time, for a little over a month, but he knew where Fifth and Vine was.

In an attempt to ensure his longevity, we're going to call the cab driver 'John Smith.' It's not his real name you understand, but to state his correct monika could possibly put his life in danger. So John Smith is the only name you're going to get.

He's twenty six years old and when not driving a cab, he's a student at James Cook University, studying botany. Plant stuff, and like most uni students his favourite plant is Ganja. The world's most loved herb.

Far North Queensland, Australia, is one of the best places on the planet to study botany. The coastal areas have some of the oldest rainforests in the world right on their doorstep, plus there's arid country just an hour or so's drive west. FNQ has two completely different ecosystems within an easy day's drive. Also, because of its remoteness, a lot of the countryside is still pristine, unspoilt by introduced plants and weeds. Perfect for the budding botanist.

John Smith has twelve months to go until he gets his PHD and then he's going to give the cab back to the guy who owns it and tell him to shove it up his arse. Until then, he needs the money. Desperately.

He has a brother, let's call him Bill. He's two years younger than John, but he's already married and has a two year old son. Bill's friends reckon he's hen pecked, but his wife has told him he isn't. And until they've changed their opinion, she's forbid him to see those friends ever again.

John and Bill's parents died in a freak boating accident three years ago and the boys were left with no other family. It's just the two of them now, plus Bill's wife and the little boy of course.

Bill loves his wife and child, and in a way John's a little envious. Currently he's very single, something which he can't see changing anytime soon. If he's not working in the taxi, he's studying or attending lectures. He doesn't have time for socialising.

He drops Jumbo's wet dream off on the corner of Fifth and Vine outside a two story building. It's an unremarkable sort of place, just a glass fronted, ground floor shop, propping up a pair of tiny, low budget apartments on the second floor. The building is an old red brick structure, decorated with what a more generous soul might describe as modern street art. To John, it's just graffiti. The shop is a pawn brokers, with a big sign across the front advertising 'Fast Loans' of the 'No credit check required' type. John drops a lot of people off at the corner of Fifth and Vine. Normally people who don't look like they could repay a favour, never mind a loan.

It's a well established cliche that Pawn Broker businesses are frequently the environment of choice for the criminal persona known as a loan shark. Such is the case once again with the Pawn Brokers on Fifth and Vine.

Recently John's brother's life became seriously enmeshed with the predator who runs those premises, and John himself will meet this unsavoury character, for the first time, a little later in our tale. But for now John has another fare to convey.

His next passenger is a young, obviously gay gentleman. He has a slender build, short pink hair and is dressed in a firm fitting purple T-shirt and a skin tight pair of gold Lycra bike pants. The man, or perhaps boy would be a more apt description, smiles incessantly and talks non stop during the fifteen minute trip to his destination. He regales John with all the tales of his life, as if John is his long lost buddy. John drops the boy at his place of residence and as his passenger hands him the fare the boy asks if he might like to come inside for a while. John smiles pleasantly and tells him thanks, going on to explain it's not his scene. He doesn't have a problem with gays, in fact, regardless of gender, John would rather meet two people who love each other, than two who hate each other any day. But despite his open mindedness, he remains steadfastly heterosexual.

It's now getting close to the end of his shift, so he heads over to his brother's place. It's a visit he's not looking forward to. Six months ago Bill did something stupid. In fact, he did something incredibly stupid, and that's why John's working all the hours he can manage. If he does, there's a slim chance Bill will make it through to the end of the year with no further impediments to his health. If he doesn't, it's a pretty safe bet Bill soon won't have any health to impede.

His wife, we shall call her Mary, is a hairdresser and has been since she began her working life as an apprentice coiffeuse seven years ago. She is also a keen jogger and a few weeks ago, she rose early one Tuesday morning, and set out on her thrice weekly run. A kilometre or so into her jog, Mary came a cropper, badly twisting her ankle on the kerb as she crossed the street. She went down quicker than a whore in knee pads and ended up in hospital with a broken tibia.

Now current fashion not withstanding, it's quite possible Mary could have spent the next thirty or so days until the cast came off, cutting hair on crutches, but her employer was not prepared to take the risk and let Mary go.

Bill works as a spare parts clerk for a large automotive dealership. The job is mildly challenging mentally, without being overly taxing, and generally Bill is content. But he's not going to attract many looks of envy by telling people how much he earns. It's not minimum wage territory, but it's not far above it.

With just one wage coming in, things were difficult. But Mr and Mrs Smith had tightened their already tight belts and soldiered on. Then the faecal material hit the rotary wind generator and their world collapsed around them. Bill and Mary's son got very sick and had to be taken to hospital.

Now in Australia we have 'Medicare'. It's a Government run, universal health care scheme, covering things like hospital fees, Doctors fees and general health expenses. But it doesn't cover everything. Some pharmaceuticals, at least the ones Master Smith required, were not covered, and were also incredibly expensive. But ever the dotting father, Bill went to see the Shylock on the corner of Fifth and Vine and borrowed a thousand bucks to pay for them. Bad move!

On the positive side, the little boy has now recovered fully, but Mary has been unable to find another job, so funds are still incredibly tight.

Initially the money lender was quite happy to let the loan accrue, but now, after five months of crippling interest repayments, the one thousand dollars has miraculously morphed into a little under two and a half grand. Bill approached the Shylock, explained he couldn't pay and asked for yet another extension. The loan shark refused and encouraged John's brother to put his accounts in order by attacking him with a pick handle. Bill nearly died from the injuries he received. His skull was fractured, his right shoulder dislocated and he now walks with a limp. According to his doctor, he probably will for the rest of his life.

It gets worse. Bill still hasn't been able to repay the loan. Now it's up to three thousand dollars and today at five thirty it's his last chance to make good.

But big brother John has a plan.

John goes to his brother's home, collects the packet he left in Bill's care earlier in the day, hugs his brother for what might be the last time, and makes his way back to the Pawn Brokers on the corner of Fifth and Vine.

He has an appointment with the money lender which he cannot avoid.

The loan shark's name is Eugene Speerwah, and in this instance at least, that name is accurate. He's a thoroughly obnoxious individual, barely deserving of the title human being.

Now the name Eugene, will probably elicit an image of a tall, weak chinned, gangly man with big ears, a prominent Roman nose, prematurely receding hair and thick lensed glasses. He would also speak fluent Klingon, his favourite piece of music would be the theme from 'Star Wars' and his five year mission would be to 'Boldly Go' to work at an electronics store everyday on the Number 57 bus. Such is not the case with Eugene Speerwah.

Speerwah is a thug. His tall, muscular body is covered with tattoos and liberal piercings. His head is shaven and his face has more metal in it that an ISIS suicide bomber. He has virtually no morals, a vicious temper and a total disregard for the law.

John Smith arrives at the corner of Fifth and Vine at four thirty as arranged and is shown through to Speerwah's office. The money lender sits behind his desk at the back of the Pawn Brokers, wearing a dark grey suit with a lighter grey shirt and a dark blue tie. As usual, he is smoking one of his expensive Cuban cigars.

John Smith introduces himself, using an alias, and presents Speerwah with a copy of a document for a term deposit bank account for twenty thousand dollars. According to the certificate the term deposit matures in six days time. The document is a fake, mocked up on Bill's home computer a few days previously.

"I need to borrow three thousand dollars for seven days," John explains, and begins to give reasons why. Speerwah couldn't give a shit. All he's interested in is the fact that the man in front of him apparently has twenty thousand dollars in the bank. Speerwah sees an opportunity of getting at least a sizeable chunk of it for himself.

38

KEVIN WILLIAM BARRY

"Sure my friend," Speerwah tells him smiling. "You've obviously got sufficient collateral to cover the loan. So all I need from you is some form of identification and then we'll go and fill out the necessary paperwork."

John nods enthusiastically, and reaches for his wallet in the back pocket of his jeans. As he pulls it out, it slips from his fingers and drops to the floor. John kneels down to retrieve it and pops back up again a moment later, looking embarrassed and apologising for his clumsiness. He hands Speerwah a fake driver's licence, bearing the name he had given the loan shark a few moments earlier, and the details of his loan are noted in a large, leather bound ledger. Five minutes later John is presented with three thousand dollars in cash. Ten minutes after that Bill enters the building on the corner of Fifth and Vine and uses the same three thousand dollars to finalize his debt with Speerwah.

Now of course, what the brothers have done is nothing more than robbing Peter to pay Paul. It's a bit like using an American Express card to pay a Visa card debt. It hasn't solved Bill's problem at all. At best, it gives them just another seven days to repay the loan. Plus another week's interest on the three grand of course.

But what has to be remembered, is this tale is more than just a story about money. It's a story about a father's love for his wife and child. It's a story about the two brothers love for each other. It's about desperation, and greed and fear for one's life and most of all, it's about revenge for the unnecessarily heinous injuries Speerwah inflicted on John's younger brother.

And it's also a little bit about botany.

Just an hours drive to the west of the city, is the town of Mareeba. The area is much drier than on the coast and in times gone by Mareeba was the centre of a very large tobacco growing district. There aren't as many farmers who still grow tobacco in the area today of course, but there are a couple, and one or two of them might be persuaded to sell a bag of 'chop chop' (Illegal tobacco) to an enterprising uni student. They might even sell such a person a few whole, dried leaves with which said student could make his own cigars.

As previously stated, closer to the coast there is a belt of dense rainforest. There's a plant which grows in this rainforest called the Gympie-gympie plant. Its botanical name is *Dendrocnide Moroides,* but the locals simply call it the 'Stinging Tree." It has large, heart shaped leaves which are covered with a multitude of tiny, hollow spines which contain one of the most insidious neurotoxins known to man. The poison is called *Moroidin* and according to a lecture John attended a few months ago, *Dendrocnide Moroides* can cause such unbearable pain it can drive a person insane. If all the tiny spines are not removed, the pain can re-occur at any time, for up to a year after the original injury. Plus the leaves can remain toxic for decades, even after they have dried out completely.

At some point after the brothers left the Pawn Brokers on the corner of Fifth and Vine, Eugene Speerwah noticed one of his treasured Cuban cigars on the floor under his desk. He couldn't remember dropping it, but assumed that he must have placed it on his desk at some time and it had rolled off onto the floor. He picked it up, dusted it off and then, using his cigar trimmer, cut the tip off. In doing so he exposed the dried Gympie-gympie leaves which had been wrapped in a casing of Tobacco. He stuck the cigar in his mouth and lit it with his solid gold 'Dunhill' lighter. He took a drag and screwed up his face in disgust. It tasted revolting. Somehow the cigar had become tainted. Perhaps it had absorbed some of the harsh chemicals the cleaner used to mop the floor, he thought. He pulled the disgusting thing out of his mouth, stubbed it out in the ashtray and dumped the lot into the metal waste paper bin next to his desk.

But it was too late. Already a few of the tiny, *Moroidin* infused spines had embedded themselves in the tip of his tongue. Within seconds his tongue began to itch and burn. The pain quickly became excruciating. Speerwah cried out in agony, but there was no one to hear his cries for help. The building was empty. Everyone else had left at the end of the working day at five thirty. Speerwah lunged for the phone and tried desperately to call for an ambulance, but the pain of his mouth was so intense he was unable to think clearly. All he could think about was the unbearable stinging. His tongue began to swell, making breathing difficult, but by this time Speerwah was in such agony he would have preferred death anyway. At least then the unbelievable torture might end. Six minutes later it did.

Partly because of the insufferable agony of his mouth and partly because he was slowly suffocating from his rapidly swelling tongue, Eugene Speerwah's heart gave out.

When one of his staff found his dead body in the morning, slumped over his desk, his face frozen in a grimace of agony, they called for an ambulance. But of course, by that time it was far too late. The coroner performed a cursory autopsy and decreed that Eugene Speerwah had most likely died of a severe allergic reaction. The swelling of his tongue had led to asphyxiation, a common cause of death in such cases. It's unlikely, but had the coroner been more thorough in his investigation he may have found minute traces of *Moroidin* in Speerwah's system. But Eugene was well known to the Police and as such, no one was keen to delve too deeply. As one of the boys in blue was heard to say. "The guys dead. Good riddance."

Speerwah had no next of kin listed in his last will and testament, so the Pawn Brokers on the corner of Fifth and Vine was sold off and the proceeds from the sale went into trust pending someone making a claim against his estate. What happened to the unpaid loans Speerwah had financed is unclear, but it is believed the ledger containing the details of those loans was purchased by someone for a few dollars during the sale of the goods and chattels associated with the business. The man who bought it was a taxi driver.

## The End

# The Trap.

*( Translated from Formosan Chinese into English with the invaluable assistance of Mr Michael Chow.)*

My name is Wai Fong. I am twenty years old. My uncle is one of the diplomats at the Taiwanese Embassy in Canberra. He's not the Ambassador you understand, just one of the diplomatic staff who live and work in the Embassy. He was kind enough to arrange a visa and a plane ticket for me so I could come to Australia and visit him. I wish he hadn't. If I'd stayed at home, I wouldn't be in the huge amount of shit I'm in now.

"You're my favourite niece," he'd told me on the phone. "I'd love for you to come and see this beautiful country. Tell my brother there will be a plane ticket waiting for you at the airport. I'll see you in eighteen days."

I could hardly wait. Ever since my uncle was posted to 'The Land Down Under', I had been dreaming of visiting that wonderfully interesting country. My uncle had spoken to my Dad on numerous occasions, always waxing lyrically about what a great country it was. It sounded like the perfect place for a young, university educated woman to take a holiday.

In high school I had learnt to speak English. All Taiwanese high school students do these days. I was far from proficient, but I knew I'd mastered it well enough to get by. Provided of course, people spoke slowly and gave me time to translate the words in my head. Reading and writing were a different matter. No matter how hard I studied, I just couldn't get my head around the totally weird symbols the Australians used in their writing. I have however, managed to memorize the way certain words look. I can for example, recognize the words for toilet- Ladies and Gents- the words Hostel and Airport. I can of course, also identify words like McDonalds and Pizza and Lager, so I knew I wasn't going to starve. Besides, many of my friends had travelled overseas, and they all told me the best thing to do was to pair up with someone who speaks English as a first language. People from Australia and England of course were always a good choice. New Zealanders, Americans and most Canadians too. Many Germans speak English well. Almost all Dutch speak and read English fluently, as do a great many French. Plus most kids doing the 'Backpacker' thing prefer to travel with a partner or in a group anyway.

I spent almost a month with my uncle and aunt in Canberra and then shrugged my backpack onto my back and caught a greyhound to Sydney. My uncle had explained that the bus would take me to the city and stop at a big, bus depot. There I would find any number of smaller buses, run by the multitude of Backpacker Hostels in Sydney, who would take me to their hostel for free if I stayed at their hostel for at least one night. He felt my plan of hooking up with another girl and travelling together was a good one. It didn't quite work out that way.

My first night in Sydney was spent at the 'Harbour View Hostel'. Although I didn't see even a hint of that city's world famous harbour. The place was both clean and tidy as well as comfortable. I was lucky, or maybe I should say unlucky, enough to meet a Dutch girl, just four months older than me, who was planning to head up the east coast of Australia in two days time. We decided to travel together.

The Dutch girls name was Vodi. She was tall and blonde, with big, round, blue eyes, pale skin and a happy smile. Unfortunately she was also a thieving bitch. Our friendship lasted only six days. By that time we hated each other. In my case at least, I felt I had good reason. Vodi stole almost all my money and spent it on drugs, and though I didn't realize until later, she'd also stolen my bus ticket. We went our separate ways on the morning of the seventeenth. Vodi left on the Greyhound at nine am, leaving me stranded in a tiny outback town called Galstone. It was there my nightmare began.

Vodi and I had been travelling by Greyhound Bus, stopping at various places which caught our interest and then moving on when we'd seen whatever there was to see. I couldn't afford to buy another bus ticket, so I decided to try my hand (thumb?) at hitch hiking. Stupid, stupid girl.

I'd met a large number of other travellers since arriving in Oz. Many of them had tried hitch hiking at some point during their travels. It was simply the cheapest way to see the country. There were, however, a few impediments to my embracing that mode of transport wholeheartedly.

One: I was by myself which made it potentially dangerous. (I'd seen 'Wolf Creek') Two: my English wasn't very good. Three: Although lots of people do it, hitch hiking is actually illegal in Australia. And four: According to the news programs I'd seen on TV over the past few nights, four young women had been attacked in the area over the last three months. They had been raped and brutally murdered.

But, on the pro hitch hiking front there were a number of factors in its favour. One: Only one bus came through Galstone each day and I'd already waved goodbye to it with my middle finger earlier that morning. Two: Thanks to the light fingered Dutch fiend, until I could get my Dad to wire me some more money, I couldn't afford a bus ticket anyway. Three: Australia is a very expensive country for a twenty year old Taiwanese University student travelling around on a shoestring budget, even if I hadn't been robbed, and hitch hiking was free. Four: Well, there wasn't a number four. I just didn't have any other choice.

Stupid, stupid, extremely stupid girl!

I heaved my backpack onto my shoulders, walked to the highway, smiled sweetly and stuck out my thumb. The first vehicle that came along, less than five minutes later, was an old and extremely dirty Toyota Land Cruiser. It pulled over. The driver looked questioningly at me and then reached over and opened the passenger door. He smiled, grunted and waved me onboard. I threw my backpack on the back seat and climbed in.

"Thank you for your kindness Sir," I said in my best English. "I wish to travel with you to the north. I am heading for Balina"

He grunted at me again, threw the car into gear and accelerated quickly, the vehicle's tyres squealing loudly on the road surface and filling the interior of the car with the smell of burning rubber.

I looked over at my new chauffeur. He was an older man, perhaps a year or two older than my father. He had long, grey, greasy hair, which he had tied back in a ponytail. His face was deeply scored and tanned by the blistering Australian sun, and his eyes were as blue as the deepest ocean. My mother would have called him handsome in a rough, unkempt sort of way. I wasn't so sure. He was dressed in a faded brown, check shirt, ancient dark blue jeans and a pair of scuffed and worn, heavy duty work boots.

"My name is Wai Fong," I told him. He ignored me.

"What is your name Sir?" I enquired. Again he ignored me. I began to feel decidedly uneasy.

"Are you going to Balina?' I asked. No response. I began to panic. Why didn't he speak?

He glanced my way and smiled. He pointed to his ear and shook his head indicating he couldn't hear me

"Oh!" I twisted around in my seat, reached over and rummaged through my backpack. I got out my well thumbed road map of the east coast of New South Wales. I tapped him on the shoulder to get his attention and pointed to the map, indicated the town of Balina, just a few centimetres south of the border with Queensland and the start of the world famous 'Gold Coast'. Sun drenched beaches, bronzed surfer guys, twenty four hour nightlife. All the things a young woman could possibly want or need for a perfect beachside holiday. "BALINA", I said loudly. He snorted with derision and waved his hands in the air. It looked like he was using sign language. Oh! He was deaf, not just hard of hearing.

Keeping one eye on the road he pointed a grubby finger at my map indicating the town of Galstone, then traced his finger along the road until it reached Coffs Harbour. He stabbed at the page a couple of times and then at himself to clarify his meaning. Then he skipped back to Galstone and once again traced the road to Coffs Harbour. He reached into his shirt pocket and pulled out a pen. He wrote '200 k' on my map and once more traced his finger from Galstone to Coffs harbour.

Then he continued on to Balina. '300 K' he wrote. I understood his meaning. He was only going as far as Coffs harbour. Balina was another three hundred kilometres further north. I nodded my thanks. I keep forgetting just how big Australia is.

We drove on in silence for about half an hour. Suddenly my new friend tapped me on the shoulder and pointed out the window towards the side of the road. There were cows grazing on the verge. Big deal. I'd seen cows before. We even have them in Taiwan. I turned and smiled at him, nodding my head to tell him I'd seen them. He grunted at me again and once more pointed urgently at the roadside. Perhaps there was something else he was wanting me to see. I turned my head and peered out the window, trying to gauge exactly what it was the man was trying to show me. I heard him rattling around for something in the side pocket of his door and then I felt a sharp pain in my thigh. I looked down to find a hypodermic syringe sticking out of my leg.

The last thing I saw before the world turned black and I passed out, was the deaf man grinning at me as if he'd just won the lottery. Shit. Looks like I'm going to be victim number five.

I WOKE UP LYING INSIDE a tent. I knew it was a tent because it was made of bright orange, waterproof polyester, it was shaped like a tent, and I was lying on top of a sleeping bag. Plus I recognised it. It was my tent. The contents of my backpack were piled neatly on the floor next to me, but my hiking boots and socks were missing. My feet were bare. My head was pounding and I was having difficulty focusing.

The front of the tent was open, allowing me to see out. I was greeted by the breathtaking vista of a beautiful, blue lake just a dozen metres from my 'doorstep'. Between the tent and the lake was a small campfire, and next to the campfire, the deaf man was hunched over, stirring something in a large, smoke blackened pot. Whatever he was cooking smelt delicious.

Gingerly I raised myself up on one elbow and edged closer to the opening, searching for an avenue of escape. My head swum and a wave of nausea washed over me. I collapsed back onto the sleeping bag and once again passed out, though this time only for a few moments. When I awoke once more, I found the man had dragged me outside. He'd propped me up against the trunk of a big iron bark tree and placed a plastic plate laden with some sort of stew near my right hand. The plastic spoon sticking out of the middle of the dish didn't look like a very practical weapon to defend myself with.

My abductor was sitting cross legged a couple of metres to my left. He was shovelling food into his mouth with a fork. He looked angry and determined.

He pointed to my brimming plate with his fork and mimed eating. Clearly he wanted me to eat the stew he had prepared. I was terrified. What the hell was going on? I started to cry.

As he couldn't speak, I surmised he had been deaf since birth. If that was the case then it was likely he could read lips. I crawled closer to him, looked him directly in the eye and begged him not to hurt me. But all he did was once again point to his ear and shake his head. He watched my lips closely however, so I was pretty sure he knew what I was saying. He also looked extremely uncomfortable.

I struggled to my feet and tried to run. I was still dizzy and the ground around the tent was uneven and strewn with large rocks. I had only taken a few steps before I fell heavily. I quickly struggled to my feet once more and ran on. The hard ground was murder on my unshod feet. Within seconds they began to hurt like I was running over broken bottles. I blotted out the pain as best I could and continued to limp painfully towards the safety of the trees. I glanced behind me. My abductor hadn't moved. He was still sitting there, slowly eating his stew, watching me hobble painfully over the stony ground. I reached the tree line and searched for some sort of trail which might lead me back to the highway. I had no idea where I was, but hurried on regardless as quickly as I could, stumbling through the dense forest. Anywhere was better than staying with a silent murderer.

Then suddenly he was standing in front of me, shaking his head as if I were some disobedient puppy who had soiled the carpet. He grabbed me by the shoulders, spun me around, back towards the campsite and pushed me forward. With no other choice I took a few steps and then collapsed to the ground. My feet were a bloody mess. They were cut to shreds.

The man reached down, wrapped one arm around my waist and lifted me over his shoulder as if I were as light as a feather. A few minutes later he dumped me back on the ground outside my tent. He picked up my dish of stew and shoved it in my hands. Then he placed his hand on top of my head and pressed down firmly. His meaning was clear. I was to stay there. I wasn't to move. My tears cascaded down my face once more. I was trapped. The deaf man was going to kill me and no one would ever find my body.

MY KIDNAPPER MADE COFFEE. Hot sweet and milky. He handed me a plastic cup, filled to the brim and then went back to where he'd been sitting and retrieved a few sheets of writing paper. He handed them to me, then turned and walked away. I watched in total confusion as he disappeared into the forest.

I looked at the pages he had given me. On them were lines and lines of writing, all of which meant nothing to me. I recognised a few of the words, but the meaning of what he had written was unfathomable. I still had no idea what the hell was going on. Was he going to come back? Was this how he killed his victims, left them stranded in the middle of the Australian bush and waited for them to starve to death?

On hands and knees I searched the area around the camp ground. There, on the other side of the campfire was a large wooden box. Inside was lots of tinned food. Meat, vegetables, potatoes, tinned fruit, plus cans of dried milk. There was a large box of breakfast cereal, tea and coffee, chocolate and other confectioneries, plus a whole gamut of other edible stuff including a dozen large bottles of water. Enough food in fact, for a whole week for two people. There were matches to relight the fire if it went out, and plenty of firewood chopped ready next to the box. Oh well, I thought, at least he doesn't want me to starve.

I crawled over to the tent and hunted through my belongings for something to use as a weapon. There was nothing more dangerous than my tooth brush. I had similar success trying to find footwear. The bastard had taken my boots plus my only other pair of shoes. He hadn't even left me with a pair of socks. I grabbed my old towel and a tracksuit top and wrapped them around my feet, tying them in place with the cord from my tracksuit pants and the belt from my good sundress. Then I hobbled down to the lake's edge and soaked my aching feet in the chilly water. I washed away the dirt and blood and inspected the damage. I had a big, but thankfully shallow cut on my left heel and my right big toe was severely lacerated. There were also numerous tiny nicks and cuts all over the soles of my feet, but nothing major. All in all I concluded, they felt much worse than they were. They hurt like hell. I rewrapped my feet and using a stout stick as a crutch, made my way back to the tent. My abductor was still nowhere to be seen.

To the east of my campsite was a small, boulder strewn hill. It was, perhaps, fifty metres high and at most a kilometre from my present position. Hopefully I would be able to see the highway from the top. I took off for the hill as fast as my aching feet would allow.

It took me over an hour of hobbling to reach the hill and climb to the top. I looked around. Everywhere I looked there was nothing but trees. Dense forest extended away in all directions, all the way to the horizon. I knew the coast must be somewhere over to the east, and in all probability, the highway was somewhere between where I was standing and the ocean. But how far? I had no idea how long had I been unconscious? I could be hundreds of kilometres inland. To try to walk out, with no shoes and only a very vague idea of where I was going would be madness. I slumped down on the ground and wept once more. I was trapped. I wasn't going anywhere and the monster who had kidnapped me knew it.

I BARELY SLEPT THAT night. I kept the fire going the whole time, building it up by dragging fallen branches and sticks over to it and throwing them on until I had a raging inferno. I figured the flames might be seen by a passing car or aircraft and at the same time keep away any dangerous animals. My kidnapper still hadn't returned by dark, so I guessed he wouldn't be back before morning. I crawled into my tent, coming back out again every time I felt the fire needed more fuel. It was a long night.

The man didn't return the next day either. I ate breakfast. Hobbled about the campsite collecting firewood. Washed myself in the lake. Made lunch. Began writing this journal and then, late in the afternoon, I had a nap. I was so exhausted I started to see dark spots before my eyes and developed a raging head ache. I slept fitfully though, always keeping one eye open, just in case the monster who had abducted me suddenly returned. He didn't. Later, as the sun sank slowly in the west, I opened a tin of of beans, heated them over the fire and sat cross legged on the edge of the lake, shovelling them into my mouth with my plastic spoon. I gasped, there on the other side of the lake was a mob of kangaroos. There was about a dozen animals. They'd come down to the water's edge to drink. They were the first kangaroos I'd seen since coming to Australia. They were a beautiful pale brown colour with darker brown stripes along their cheeks. The stood up tall, watching me from the opposite bank and then, realising I wasn't a threat, dropped their heads and resumed drinking.

I became angry then. My campsite was in a beautiful place, filled with wonderful and interesting wild life. I'd seen Kangaroos, Kookaburras, the big lizards the Aussies called a Goanna and all manner of birdlife. I'd even seen an Emu. To camp at such a glorious, secluded spot should have been a wonderful experience. Instead I was terrified, lost and alone and fearing for my life. I'd been drugged, kidnapped, injured and subjected to utter terror by a rapist and a murderer, and all because I'd been foolish enough to befriend a thief who'd stolen all my money, forcing me to hitch hike.

The second night of my ordeal was entirely different to the first. Early in the evening the clouds rolled in from the west. They were thick and black and swirled viscously, like an inverted cauldron of boiling oil. Lightning flashed with fearsome intensity in the distance and thunder boomed across the sky. Around 8:00 pm the heavens opened and the rain came down in huge silver sheets. I'd never seen such a heavy downpour. The sound of the rain drumming on the roof of my little tent was almost deafening. It continued to bucket down until around midnight when the rain finally began to ease.

When I awoke the next morning, the sun was once again blazing brilliantly in the sky and there was little sign of the deluge of the previous night. The ground and the trees around my campsite were wet of course, but there was no sign of flooding and none of my essential food or equipment had washed away.

But the fire had been well and truly swamped.

At first I wasn't too concerned about the fire. I would eat cold cereal for breakfast and there was fresh fruit for lunch, plus I could manage without a hot meal at night. But, there was that all important need to attract attention. If I was going to make it back to civilization alive, I needed to keep my signal fire burning. I wasted half a box of matches trying to get the damp kindling to light before I finally realized I was fighting a losing battle. I needed something dry, something which would burn easily until the kindling dried out. I could use the pages from my diary, but I wanted to keep the record of my abduction intact. If I died, my parents and the people who loved me would need to know what had happened. This meant I had to keep the journal whole and had to leave it where someone would find it.

My other option was to use the pages my abductor had left with me. No doubt the words he'd written there were important to him. But I couldn't read them anyway. They were in English. I laid the damp kindling in the sun to dry and then, late in the afternoon, I put a match to the pages and carefully fed the resulting flame with small bits of wood, gradually placing each piece on top, so I didn't smother the flame. Soon I had a raging fire blazing once more.

As I'd hoped my signal fire finally attracted someone's attention. Unfortunately it attracted the wrong person.

It was just two hours before dusk when a slightly built man with a rucksack on his back walked into the clearing. He was around fifty years of age, with scrawny arms and legs, a prominent nose and a weak chin. His thinning hair was plastered to his head with sweat and his clothes were rank with filth. There was a bright red scar slashed across his forehead, He took one look at me, threw down his rucksack and began to chuckle insidiously. Suddenly he rushed towards me, screaming obscenities. He grabbed me and threw me to the ground. He jumped on top of me. Pining me down as he tried to tear the clothes from my body. He grabbed my left breast and squeezed it painfully, making me cry out in pain. It was then I realized that this man, not my abductor, was the person responsible for the rape and murder of the four young girls I'd heard about. He was about to make me number five.

My attacker raised himself up on one elbow as he tried to extricate himself from his pants. He looked down at me and leered. There was a sickening thud, like someone had hit a watermelon with a baseball bat and the evil little man was thrown sideways. Standing there in the gathering twilight was my abductor. In his hand he carried a blood soaked axe. The rapist was surely dead, and yet the deaf guy dragged him off me and in a frenzy of unbelievable violence struck his victim again and again with his axe until the man's head was nothing but a bloody pulp. Then he grabbed him by the ankle and dragged him off into the forest.

I should have jumped to my feet and quickly run as far away from that horrific carnage as possible. But I was frozen by the trauma of the rapist's attack. I was unable to move.

Moments later the deaf man returned from disposing of his victim's body. He picked up his axe and hurled it as far as he could into the lake, then staggered down to the water's edge and dove in, fully clothed. He quickly began to wash the blood and gore from his body. After a few minutes he clambered out again, strode purposefully to my tent and crawled inside. He came out seconds later with a pair of my jeans and a t-shirt. He handed them to me and pointed to the lake. I realised that I too was splattered with gore.

As I sat on the gravel at the waters edge washing my attackers blood and brains from my body, the deaf man hurried around the campsite, packing away all my possessions and stuffing them in my backpack. He quickly disassembled my tent, rolled it up tightly and strapped it to the rucksack. Then he went over to the food box and dragged it to one side. Underneath, hidden in a shallow hole in the ground, were my hiking boots and socks. When I'd finished washing and had dressed in clean clothes, he handed them to me and waited while I put them on. Then he heaved my backpack onto his shoulders, gently took my hand and led me into the forest.

It took only ten minutes or so of trekking through the trees before we reached his old Toyota Land Cruiser. He'd hidden it from view under a canopy of fallen branches. To the casual observer it was virtually invisible. He dragged away the branches, opened the passenger side door and beckoned me in. Then he went around to his side, clambered in and started the ancient vehicles diesel. Half an hour later we were back at the highway. He stopped at the intersection and turned right, back towards Galstone.

Suddenly he pulled over, stopped the car by the side of the road and turned off the motor. He sat there silently for several long moments. Then his head sank forward slowly until his forehead rested on the steering wheel. He let out a low cry like a wounded animal and began to cry. The tears poured from his eyes, dripping wetly onto the legs of his jeans, once again soaking the fabric.

Half an hour later we stopped again, this time just outside a tiny graveyard on the outskirts of Galstone. He climbed out of the car, walked around to my side and opened the door. Gently he took my had and led me through the cemetery, to a grave over near the back fence. The words on the headstone read:

Elizabeth McCullough.

1$^{st}$ November 2001 - 3$^{rd}$ March 2017

and then some other words I couldn't understand.

The deaf man reached into his back pocket and pulled out his wallet. He opened it and showed me a photo of himself and a dark haired, slim woman about the same age. They were standing either side of a young girl with their arms wrapped around her. There was a birthday cake with the number 16 written on it in blue icing. She was just sixteen years old.

I looked up at Mr McCullough. Once again there were tears in his eyes. I faced him so he could see my lips.

"He murdered your daughter?" I asked, pointing back down the highway towards the camp ground with one hand, and drawing my finger across my forehead, were the rapists scar had been with the other, so it was perfectly clear to Elizabeth's father who I was talking about.

He nodded sadly. I'd finally guessed what the past three days had been all about. The rapist and murderer had been in the area before. Elizabeth McCullough had been a victim of some earlier killing spree. Of course, I now wished I hadn't burnt the letter he had written for me. No doubt those pages would have explained what he was planning and would have answered some of the unanswered questions I still had; like how exactly he had lured his daughter's killer to the secluded campsite? In fact, all I knew for certain, was that the whole thing had never been about me.

I'd just been the bait.

We reached Galstone just as the last rays of the dying sun dipped down behind the hills to the west of the tiny town. Mr McCullough drove down Main Street, did a U-turn and parked the old Land Cruiser outside a modern looking, red brick building. The place was lit up brightly, and through the large sliding glass doors at the front of the building, I could see a man in uniform working diligently behind a chest high counter. On the front of the building was an oval, blue and white, neon sign. On it was another word I recognised. POLICE. Mr McCullough reached across and pushed open my door. He nodded, letting me know it was okay for me to get out, then he unclipped his seatbelt and started to open his own door. It seemed he was going to turn himself in.

He was right to do that of course. He'd taken the law into his own hands. He'd killed the man who had murdered his daughter. Plus he'd abducted me, drugged me, left me stranded, terrified and alone in the middle of nowhere. Now it seemed, although he'd set out to extract a terrible vengeance on the man who'd slain his daughter, he'd fully understood there would be a price to be paid after he'd done so. He understood that society would want their pound of flesh.

But hadn't the man sitting next to me already suffered enough? I can't even begin to comprehend the utter, soul destroying grief felt by parents who have lost a child. How much more devastating must it have been for Elizabeth's father, knowing that his daughter, his child, his baby, had been murdered by an insane sex fiend?

The man who had attacked me deserved to die. Of that I was certain. I was now also sure that I had never been in any real danger. I'm convinced Mr McCullough was watching over me the whole time, just waiting for that insane bastard to show up so he could kill him.

My damaged feet would heal quickly. Not so the broken heart of my new friend. Surely that was more than a pound of flesh. It was for me. Society could go to hell.

As he turned to climb out of the car, I reached over and gently touched his shoulder. He turned back to me and I shook my head, telling him no, don't do this. I rummaged through my backpack and pulled out my well worn map of the east coast of New South Wales. I pointed at our current location, the tiny town of Galstone, then traced my finger northwards, along the highway, two hundred kilometres, to the city of Coffs harbour. The place where, three days ago, he'd told me he lived. I tapped the spot emphatically. I made sure he could see my lips.

"Take me there." I said. "That's were we should go."

He nodded sadly, then started the car. We said goodbye to each other three hours later.

# *The End*

# Once Bitten, Twice Shy

*A short story*
*by*
*Kevin William Barry*
*Reading Instructions:*
*Place tongue firmly in cheek when reading this short story*

S he told me it was to be a gift. As if she expected me to be pleased I'd just been told she was going to make me immortal and that such declarations were common place and not just the weird ravings of a mad woman.

I'D ALWAYS KNOWN EVELYN was a bit strange, but I guess love made me blind to exactly how strange. The first time I met her I was instantly swept away by her beauty. Her flawless alabaster skin, her lionesque mane of dark, auburn hair, her piercing blue eyes and voluptuous curves. She was beyond beautiful. She was sexy, sultry, enigmatic and to my eyes at least, totally irresistible.

That first time I met her was on a Thursday evening. I'd been working late, tidying up a few loose ends and polishing my closing address for the case I'd been defending for the last nineteen days. I was due to present my closing argument to the jury on Monday and to be honest I didn't like my chances. From a professional point of view I wasn't happy about that- no lawyer likes to lose a case, especially such a high profile one. But from a personal perspective I didn't mind so much. The bastard was as guilty as hell and in my heart at least, my sense of righteousness usurped the obligation I had to provide my client with a robust and comprehensive legal defence. But that didn't mean I hadn't given it my best shot, I always do. It's just that in this instance, a ruling against my client wasn't going to keep me awake at night worrying about the injustice of it all.

I'd just put the desktop computer to sleep and was preparing to go home when there was a hesitant tap on the frosted glass panel of my outer office door. Brenda, my indispensable office girl, had already left for the day so I called out, "Come in. Doors open," and in an instant my life changed forever.

Evelyn Rau eased open the door and moved into my office like a dancer, her dainty, high heeled clad feet seemed to float over the office's highly polished timber flooring with barely a touch. She was dressed in black, in a form fitting dress which almost touched the ground at the back, but which was cut away at the front, in a wide, truncated vee, to reveal her pale, yet shapely legs. The top part of her dress featured a high collar, with a plunging neckline to make the most of her considerable cleavage, but her arms and shoulders were covered. The stark contrast between the shiny black material of her dress and the ivory curves of her breasts and legs, together with the 'fuck me heels' somehow made her look even more sensual than if she'd been naked.

She drifted closer to my desk and held out her hand, introduced herself in a soft, sultry voice, slightly accented and vaguely reminiscent of some ancient, middle European country. She apologized for calling unannounced and so late in the evening.

"My name is Evelyn," she told me in a breathless whisper. "Evelyn Rau. I need to engage the services of an accomplished legal council. I have been falsely accused of murder and although my court appointed lawyer has done his best, he is little better than an incompetent fool.

I have been told you have considerable experience in such criminal matters and that you might be available to take me on as a client."

Of course, under normal circumstances, I would have been annoyed at the unconventional way in which Miss Rau had approached me. She should have phoned during office hours, made an appointment with Brenda, perhaps given my assistant some details of her arrest and allowed me sufficient time to make a few inquiries of the arresting officer and the detective assigned to the case. But I was dazzled by Evelyn's beauty and charm, so I foolishly forgave the unorthodox way in which she had thrust herself into my life. I smiled, invited her to take a seat and urged her to tell me how she came to be charged with such a heinous crime.

She smiled shyly, revealing dazzlingly white teeth between full, blood red lips, and perched her curvaceous bottom on the edge of the leather office chair on the opposite side of my desk. I reached into a drawer and pulled out a large notepad and my gold plated fountain pen. The Parker had been a gift from my parents, presented to me on the day I passed the bar exam a little over five years ago. My father had died of a heat attack just seven months later, so the old fashioned pen has become a treasured memento. In fact, it's more valuable to me than any other single item in my possession.

"So tell me Miss Rau," I urged. "What are the details of the case against you?"

Over the next hour Evelyn explained how she had been arrested for the brutal slaying of a homeless man, six nights ago, on the banks of the Brisbane River. The victim's name was Alfred Winster. He was fifty seven. He had no regular income, no permanent place of residence and no discernible next of kin. Although he didn't have a criminal record, other than the occasional drunk and disorderly conviction, he was well known to the police, and was a regular attendant at a number of church run soup kitchens and homeless shelters in the city. He'd been stabbed in the neck with a razor sharp implement, severing his carotid artery, and had died of massive blood loss. A witness had seen a woman answering Evelyn's description kneeling beside Winster's body. The young man had confronted the woman, yelling at her, questioning what the hell she was doing and the woman had run off. The police had brought in tracker dogs which led them directly to Evelyn's apartment just a few streets away. Miss Rau had claimed she'd been in bed asleep, but when the cops searched her home, they'd found a long black skirt and blouse in Evelyn's laundry hamper. Both items of clothing were soaked in blood. Forensic evidence had proven conclusively that the blood was Winster's. Soil samples taken from the soles of her shoes compared favourably with those from the river bank, and this, together with other forensic evidence, had positively confirmed Evelyn had definitely been the woman seen at the scene of the crime.

All of which posed the inescapable question. How the hell do I defend Evelyn Rau against such insurmountable and seemingly overwhelming evidence?

"The police seem to have a pretty damning case against you, Miss Rau," I told her. "Do you have any explanation for that?"

She stared at the floor, shaking her head sadly.

"I'm afraid I have been most foolish. I was walking home along the river bank when I heard someone cry out in terror. I saw two men fighting. One man was tall and heavily built. He was bald and his muscular body was covered in a multitude of tattoos. Suddenly he had a knife in his hand, I saw the blade flashing in the moonlight and the smaller of the two men fell to the ground. The bald man ran off and I went to the injured man's aid. I tried to stop the bleeding, but there was nothing I could do. He died before I could get help. Then someone yelled at me, asked me what I was doing and I panicked. I knew it looked as if I was the one who had attacked him. So I ran away."

"And when the police came to your apartment, you decided to claim you knew nothing about the murder," I offered

"Exactly. Now I realize I've been extremely stupid. I should have just told the truth. But I was terrified they would think it was I who had murdered that poor man. Can you help me? Please say that you can."

I imagine most women would have broken down at that point, burst into tears or maybe even become hysterical. Evelyn Rau however, was made of sterner stuff. But I could still tell that behind the facade, she was beside herself with worry.

"I'll certainly do my best," I told her. "The fact you're sitting in this office tells me your previous, court appointed lawyer, has already arranged bail for you?" Evelyn nodded. "Good. I'm busy in court until three tomorrow afternoon, but after that I can devote some time to your case. The first thing you need to do is go to the police and change your story. Explain to them that you panicked and that's why you lied. From now on you must be one hundred percent truthful. They won't just take your word for it of course, but at least you will have a plausible reason for your deceit. Then you have to go to the court and arrange for me to represent you rather than your legal aid lawyer. I can't do anything until you make my appointment official."

Just to make sure she understood perfectly the financial ramifications of that appointment, I told her, "I'm sorry Miss Rau, unlike your court appointed lawyer, my services are not covered by 'Legal Aid. They're not free." Then I went on to discuss my fee structure, and once she'd agreed to it, I had Evelyn sign a contract for me to represent her. She smiled and shook her head in amazement when I mentioned my hourly figure, as if such an amount was totally insignificant. As our association progressed, I was to learn that for the beautiful Miss Rau, my fee for service rate, an amount most found quite expensive, was little more than pocket change. Evelyn Rau was not only beautiful, she was also very rich. In fact she was incredibly rich.

I WAS DUE TO MEET MISS Rau, for the second time, at eleven Monday morning. So I was surprised when my cell phone chirped at me late Saturday evening.

"I have your fountain pen," Evelyn Rau announced in her husky, middle European accented voice. "I must have used it when we signed our contract and put it in my handbag by mistake. I am so dreadfully sorry. You must have been very worried about misplacing such a beautiful writing implement. I am nearby, perhaps you will allow me to return it to you."

I hadn't noticed the pen was missing. I don't use it regularly, only when I'm in the office, never when in court where I might lose it. I explained that I was at my home, not in the office, and asked her to just bring it with her on Monday.

"But I feel so bad about taking it," she said. "Please allow me to return it to you immediately. I will not sleep tonight from worrying if I don't. Besides, I am already near your home."

Looking back on that night, there were a number of things that should have set alarm bells ringing. For example, my cell phone number is unlisted and I'm certain I hadn't given it to Miss Rau. Similarly, my home address isn't in the book. Also, I'm pretty sure the first time we met, Evelyn wasn't carrying a handbag. So the only way she could have taken my fountain pen was by hiding it on her person or carrying it in her hand. Not something someone would do 'by mistake.' But at the time those things simply didn't occur to me. Even then the stunning Miss Rau already had me under her spell. I'd barely uttered the word "Okay" when she hung up. Just minutes later there was a knock on my door. When I opened it, Evelyn stood on my threshold dressed in a long black overcoat, clinched tightly around her tiny waist and closed firmly against the cold winter night. Her feet were encased in stylish black ankle boots and she wore black leather gloves, trimmed with soft grey fur.

"Well, aren't you going to invite me in?" she asked smiling.

I know I should have turned her away, just taken back my fountain pen and wished her good night. I should have told her I would see her Monday as arranged, and left it at that. But I didn't. Of course I didn't. But I must have acted hesitantly because Evelyn suddenly became very upset and began apologising for being so thoughtless.

"I am so sorry for calling so unexpectedly once again. It's just that I am only recently arrived in your wonderful country and I am yet to make any real friends. I was hoping perhaps we could go for a drink or something. I understand that as I am your client, perhaps you will consider such actions to be inappropriate. But I have been so terribly lonely since arriving here and you seem like such a nice man."

What could I say? She was right of course. The proper thing for me to do was to send her away. Starting a personal relationship with a current client was madness. But as I looked into her sad, piercing blue eyes, my heart melted. I stepped to the side and invited her in.

"Sure Miss Rau. Please come in. I have a bottle of passably good red here somewhere. Perhaps you'd care for a glass?"

She glided into the room and began to unbuckle her overcoat. She slipped it from her shoulders and passed it to me to hang up. Underneath she wore a short black dress with a high collar. Her shoulders were bare and the dress was backless almost to her waist. I was beginning to think my new friend and client liked black.

She glided over to the living room's huge French window, overlooking the twinkling lights of the city, and gazed out at the spectacular view of Brisbane while I went into the kitchen to get us the wine. When I returned she was still standing there, transfixed by the sight of the river as it meandered its way through the still bustling metropolis. I knew what she was thinking. It had been right there, just to the left of the GIO building, under the freeway. That was where Mr Winster had been killed. Somewhere out there in the night was his killer, and unless the cops found him, Evelyn Rau was going to go to prison for a murder she had not committed. Although I couldn't be certain, I imagine that unless they received further evidence of someone else's culpability, they probably won't even bother looking.

Evelyn and I took our wine into the lounge room and sat together on the couch. For the next three hours we chatted like old friends. It seemed her claim she just wanted someone to talk to was accurate, as we didn't discuss her case once. I learnt that she had recently moved to Australia from Hungary, was 'independently wealthy' and was remotely related to to royalty. Or at least she had been.

"In fact," she said laughing, "if it were not for the demise of the Hungarian monarchy, a little over one hundred years ago, you would have to address me as 'Countess'. In more recent times my family is still well regarded. My father held a position high up in the communist party, and when the wall came down and we were no longer part of the Soviet Union, he used his influence to amass a considerable fortune. Of course, all that happened many years before I was born.... But I am being rude. I have spoken about myself enough. Please tell me about yourself. I suppose you know you have a very famous surname."

I rolled my eyes. Yes, I knew my family name was noteworthy. I had been teased about it when I was in school, and barely a day went by when someone didn't make a joke about it. I'd briefly considered changing it, but my father was proud of our Dutch heritage and when he died, it had seemed disloyal or disrespectful to change it. I have to admit though, it was better than being called Hitler.

"You know he was just a character in a book don't you? He never really existed." I said.

Evelyn laughed at my discomfort, placed her hand on my leg and gave it a friendly squeeze. "Oh you silly man," she giggled. "Of course he did."

IT WAS GETTING CLOSE to two am before Evelyn said goodnight. I must admit I hadn't enjoyed anyone's company so much in a very long time. I'd found our conversations both spirited and entertaining, and even though I was physically tired, I didn't want the night to end. She seemed reluctant too, but inevitably all good things must come to a close, so I called her a cab. As I said goodnight at the door she drew me into her arms and hugged me.

"Goodnight my lovely new friend," she whispered. Then she kissed me on the cheek and left.

The next time I saw Evelyn was Monday night. She'd phoned me at the office early Monday morning and asked if she could reschedule our meeting for later in the day as she had to attend to some urgent business in Sydney. I reminded her that the conditions of her bail would preclude her from travelling interstate, but she simply laughed my warning off as if such things as travel restrictions were unimportant.

"I will be back in Brisbane by six this evening. Besides, I will be travelling in my own private jet, so the police won't even know I have been away. Perhaps we can meet at your home and discuss things later this evening. Shall we say.....seven thirty."

Before I could object Evelyn had hung up and when I tried to ring her back to discuss a more appropriate time and place, I found she had rung from an unlisted number. I tried the cell phone number she'd given me, but it just rang out, unanswered, and without giving me the option of leaving a message.

I shrugged. Once again I should have been annoyed at her selfish, not to mention foolish antics, but the truth was I was glad we would be meeting in private. I had Brenda ring the catering company my law firm occasionally used and arranged for a sumptuous dinner for two to be delivered to my home address at seven. I'm quite an accomplished cook, but as I was expecting to be extremely busy in the office right up until after six that evening, I thought it prudent to leave dinner in the hands of the professionals. It was much easier to simply put the dishes in the oven on a low heat until we were ready to eat.

Next I rang the Roma Street police station and asked to speak to
Detective Inspector Roger Dark. DI Dark was the officer investigating
the murder of Alfred Winster and I needed him to email me a copy
of the transcript of Evelyn's interrogation together with other witness
statements and evidence lists. I'd had dealings with Roger before and
knew him to be a straight shooter. Some cops try to make it difficult
for defence lawyers, but luckily for me, DI Dark wasn't one of them. I'd
had copies of everything pertaining to the case so far e-mailed to me by
two thirty that afternoon. What I found was quite disturbing.

Saturday night, or perhaps early Sunday morning, a second man
had been found dead on the banks of the Brisbane river. Once again the
victim had been a homeless man. Once again he'd had his carotid artery
severed and had bled to death. This time there had been no witnesses
to the murder and when, as a matter of course, the cops had checked
Evelyn's whereabouts, she was not at home and did not answer her cell
phone.

Needless to say, unless he'd been killed after two am Sunday
morning, the fact she was with me, at my apartment Saturday night,
precluded her from being responsible for this second murder. That gave
me reason to suspect my initial assumption- that Evelyn was innocent-
had been correct.

But what if this second victim had been killed later than two am?
The man's autopsy was inconclusive on that score. The closest the
coroner could guess at was some time between midnight and four am.
That meant Evelyn was still in the picture. Was my new friend Evelyn
Rau some sort of serial killer? Was she a mad woman, hell bent on
ridding the city of its homeless population?

I spent the rest of the day studying every facet of Evelyn's case. I
read everything sent to me twice, took copious amounts of notes, and
rang both the Hungarian Embassy and the Australian Department of
Immigration in an attempt to glean as much information as I could
about the sultry, enigmatic Miss Rau. Then I sent an e-mail to a firm

of private investigators I knew of in Budapest, and asked them to make inquiries with the local police. In addition to the background check, I wanted them to see if there had been any murders over the past few years in Hungary, with a similar MO as the two here in Oz.

Around three thirty Brenda stuck her head around my door and told me she was finishing up for the day. She was taking her annual holidays at the end of the month, intending to go to Airlie Beach and the beautiful Whitsunday Islands for three weeks. She needed to buy herself some new swimwear and other bits and bobs for the trip so was taking an early mark. I left the office myself a couple of hours later.

IT GETS DARK AROUND six in Brisbane during the winter, so by the time I arrived home the sun had already dropped below the horizon and the night sky was ablaze with the twinkling of stars and a huge silver orb of the full moon. It was nearly seven. I took the stairs to my apartment two at a time and hurried inside. I bolted into the bathroom, stripped off my office clothes and stepped into the shower. Ten minutes later I was squeaky clean, freshly shaved and dressed casually in jeans and a t-shirt. My cleaning lady comes on a Monday so the place was immaculate for once. All that was left for me to do was wait for the caterers to deliver diner and then sit tight until Evelyn arrived at seven thirty.

To my surprise I was as excited as a schoolboy at the prospect of seeing her again. More than once I caught sight of my reflection in the darkened glass of the French doors leading out onto the balcony, to find myself grinning like a loon. With a start I realised Evelyn's charm had cast a spell over me. After just one pseudo date, I was rapidly falling in love with her. My heart was racing. One second I was on a high, picturing us together in my minds eye, happily enjoying our love for each other. The next I felt nauseous, a feeling of dread washing over me, as I contemplated the very real possibility that my love for her would not be reciprocated. What would I do if she didn't love me in return?

At seven thirty precisely, the recently identified woman of my dreams knocked on the door. With a lump in my throat big enough to choke an elephant, I cautiously opened the door and let her in.

Once again she was dressed in her black overcoat. This time though, when she slipped it from around her shoulders, she revealed a long flowing silk dress, split from the floor almost to her waist at the side and with a plunging neckline which did little to hide the delightful curves of her full and obviously unsupported breasts. Not one to fly in the face of tradition, once again her beautiful garment was black.

"Good evening my dear friend," she greeted me, smiling as if I had just told her she had won a million dollars. "Thank you for inviting me once again into your home."

She followed me into the kitchen and as I prepared us both a drink, she told me, in vague terms, about her business trip to Sydney.

"Listen Evelyn," I interrupted her. "I have to tell you there has been a new development in your case. The police have found another body. Once again the victim was a homeless man. He was killed down by the river, but a few kilometres further upstream from the first victim. They found him early Sunday morning. The killer used the same MO. The cops are pretty certain it's the same killer."

Evelyn looked horror stricken. "Oh no. Not another one. How awful." But then the same thought I'd had occurred to her. "But I was here with you Saturday night until after two in the morning. Surely that proves I couldn't have killed him?"

I smiled encouragingly. "Well, of course I'm certain you didn't murder either one of them. And from the cop's perspective, the fact you were here Saturday night certainly makes it look less likely. But we're not out of the woods yet. The second victim's actual time of death isn't perfectly clear. He could have been killed sometime after two. That's after you left here."

Evelyn nodded thoughtfully, twirling the stem of the wine glass I had just handed her without drinking and considering the ramifications of what I'd just told her.

Of course, by now I'd convinced myself Evelyn was innocent. I told her as much and then led her back into the lounge room where we continued our discussion. Over the next half hour or so we discussed what we should do next. The most important, most urgent matter on our agenda was finding the muscular, heavily tattooed, bald man Evelyn had seen attacking Mr Winster. That was imperative.

On the one hand, although Evelyn had already provided a vague description to the cops, and had laboriously gone through seemingly endless mugshots of known criminals, it was unlikely the police would put much credence in her story. We simply couldn't expect them to dedicate many man hours searching for her mysterious killer if they didn't really believe he existed. On the other hand, the murderer had struck twice in less than a week and as such, statistics told us when that happened, the killer was much more likely to strike again sooner rather than later. With luck, when he did, someone else would be on the scene to substantiate Evelyn's story and be able to provide the cops with a more detailed description of the 'Perp'. Hopefully one which would lead to an arrest.

But we couldn't rely on that happening purely by chance. We had to increase our odds somehow. There was a firm of private investigators whom I had used in the past. They normally provided my company with surveillance services and the like. They were reasonably inexpensive so I suggested we engage a few of their men to act as bait. We'd have them dress as homeless men and have them wander along the more secluded sections of the banks of the Brisbane river late at night, hoping to draw Winster's killer out. Of course, we'd have to arm them with taizers and other means of self defence. We didn't want to be responsible for anyone getting hurt. We'd also have to provide them with two-way radios so that they could call for back up in the event of an attack. It wasn't a fool proof plan, but off the top of my head, I couldn't think of a better, more workable one. Evelyn smiled and nodded in agreement. It was decided I would contact the private investigation company first thing in the morning.

"So," I said rubbing my hands together to indicate the business part of our evening was at an end. "I have dinner keeping warm in the oven for us. I hope you're hungry."

"Oh Darling," Evelyn exclaimed, "I'm so sorry. I hope you didn't go to too much trouble. I have already eaten. I didn't know you were going to cook. I'm sorry, I couldn't eat another bite. I'm completely full..... But you go ahead and eat. I'll just sip on my wine while I keep you company."

I asked her if she was sure she wasn't even just a little bit peckish, but she insisted she wasn't hungry. I on the other hand, was starving. Once again she urged me to eat, so I went into the kitchen and took both meals out of the oven. One I took into the dining room and placed on a place mat on my rosewood dining table, the other I left to cool, intending to put it in the freezer once it had cooled.

The lobster was delicious and as I ate Evelyn watched me in silence, smiling and occasionally lifting her wine glass to her lips for a tiny sip. She obviously wasn't much of a drinker, I'd noticed last time she'd barely touched her wine.

"Can I ask you a question?" I asked as I approached the final mouthfuls.

"Of course."

"Do you call all your friends 'Darling'?"

She treated me to another one of her time altering smiles. "No, only the ones I've fallen desperately in love with," she replied. Then she stood up from her seat, crossed over to my side of the table, and kissed me. Her kiss was soft and cool yet filled with almost unbearable passion and longing. She took her mouth away from mine and stepped back. Then she lifted her hands to her throat and unclipped the clasp of her dress. The silky black fabric slipped down her body to pool at her feet. She was totally, beautifully, magnificently naked underneath.

"Come on darling," she commanded, floating lazily towards my bedroom. "Let me show you how to make love Hungarian style."

OUR FIRST NIGHT TOGETHER was beyond anything I'd experienced ever before. Our love making was passionate, urgent and extremely physical. The sex was almost primal. At one stage Evelyn actually growled quietly, like some sexy wild animal, she was so caught up in the throws of our passion. When our lust for each other was sated, Evelyn fell asleep in my arms. I watched her sleeping, her breathing slow and rhythmic in the moon light. She was the most beautiful woman I had ever met, and I couldn't believe she was mine. Although we barely knew each other, she'd told me she loved me. Desperately, in fact.

I must have fallen asleep sometime later and when I awoke, Evelyn was gone. There was a note, written in her dainty, highly ornate hand, laying next to my pillow. It said simply, "See you tomorrow night, my love. E." I smiled to myself and drifted off to sleep once more.

But when I woke again the next morning I found a number of things which were most confusing. Firstly, Evelyn's dress was still where she had dropped it on the lounge room floor. Also her coat was hanging on the coat hook on the back of the kitchen door, where I had put it the previous evening. Most strange was the fact the deadlock on the front door was still engaged. The key was still in the lock and there was no way she could have locked the door from the outside without it. I discovered the French doors out onto the balcony were slightly ajar, but I live on the fourteenth floor, and unless my new girlfriend was into climbing down the sides of buildings, in the nude, I couldn't work out how the hell she had left.

I was totally confused, but I was also late for work. I made a quick phone call to Evelyn's cell, which predictably went unanswered as I rushed around the kitchen preparing my breakfast, and then tried again fifteen minutes later just before heading for the shower. No luck there either.

When I got to the office just before eight thirty, my PA Brenda was, as always, already hard at it.

"Good morning David," she greeted me smiling. "There's an e-mail from the investigators in Hungary in your in-box, one from the Department of Immigration, and a couple of others from DI Dark. He's phoned twice already this morning. He said he was on his way out, so he might be hard to get hold of until later in the day. In the meantime, apparently the e-mails give details of what he wants to discuss. Uh, everything else is of lesser importance."

I thanked Brenda, went into my office and powered up my computer. I opened the office e-mail account and that was when things became even more confusing. The first piece of correspondence was from Szucs and Associates, the Hungarian private investigation firm I had do a back ground check on Evelyn for me. Their response was quite an eye opener.

As a condition of her parole, Evelyn had been required to surrender her passport. DI Dark had given me that document's number and I had forwarded it on to Szucs and Associates. According to the Hungarian Department of Immigration, Evelyn Rau's passport had been cancelled a little over three months ago. The reason given was that Miss Rau was deceased. WHAT? Further investigation revealed that Evelyn Rau had been murdered by person or persons unknown. Not only that, details of that murder mirrored almost exactly, the two murders my new girlfriend was accused of. The e-mail also included a number of photographs, borrowed from the friends and relatives of the woman the Hungarian authorities claimed the passport belonged to. She was blonde, at least thirty kilos heavier than my girl and perhaps a decade older. There was other stuff as well, all of it leaving me in no doubt, the girl I knew as Evelyn Rau and the Hungarian woman the Szucs guys were investigating, weren't the same person. That could only mean one of two things. Either there'd been a stuff up with the passport numbers, or my Evelyn had stolen the real Evelyn Rau's identity. If that second scenario was the case, it seemed likely she had murdered her to do it?

The second e-mail was from the Australian Department of Immigration. They claimed they had no record of anyone named Evelyn Rau entering the country over the past six months. They also had no record of Evelyn's passport number anywhere in their data bank. That meant Evelyn, or whoever she really was, had entered the country illegally.

The third e-mail was one of the e-mails from DI Dark. This first one he'd sent around eight last night. Ostensibly it was just more information pertaining to Evelyn's case and added little to the mystery I now found myself involved in. But the forth piece of correspondence, the second e-mail from DI Dark which he'd sent at seven twenty two this morning, had me in a lather. Now there was a third victim. He was a young university student who also worked as a doorman at one of Brisbane's premier night clubs. He'd been set upon in the early hours of the morning as he walked home along the banks of the Brisbane river. The young man was fit and quite handy in a scrap and although he had been badly injured, he'd been able to fight off his attacker. He'd survived. He'd described his assailant as female, around 173 cm tall, with pale skin and auburn hair. He also said she was incredibly strong and behaved quite manic in her attack. "She tried to bite me, almost as if she was possessed by some sort of insane, wild animal," the victim had told Roger.

There now seemed little doubt that Evelyn, or whatever my new girlfriend's real name was, was the culprit behind the spate of murders DI Dark was investigating. I dialled his number immediately. Luckily I caught him at his desk.

Now as far as I'm concerned, client confidentiality doesn't mean squat when peoples lives are likely to be at risk, so I gave him all the information I'd gleaned from my people in Budapest, plus the stuff from the Australian Department of Immigration. I also told him about Evelyn's claim that she had her own private jet and gave him her cell phone number, explaining that I had tried numerous times without success to reach her.

"Yea. That's the same number we have on file here," Roger told me. "I've tried to contact her myself any number of times and even put a GPS trace on the phone. But it looks as if she might have switched it off and taken the battery out. Thanks for the private jet info. We're already watching the main carriers out of Brisbane airport. I'll get on to the smaller airports now too. Hopefully she hasn't already flown the coop."

We discussed the case further, swapping bits of intel when we could and then Roger hung up. I spent the rest of the day trying unsuccessfully to track Evelyn down. Perhaps it was ego, or perhaps my love for her just wouldn't allow me to believe what I knew to be true. I simply found it impossible to credit those heinous crimes to the beautiful creature I had come to worship and adore so much. There had to be another solution. I worked tirelessly trying to find her until well after eight that evening before finally calling it a day. In the back of my mind I secretly hoped that Evelyn would be waiting for me when I returned to my apartment. I prayed that she'd be able to explain what the hell was going on and that it was all just a big misunderstanding. It would be six days, or rather nights, before I saw her again.

ANYONE WHO WORKS IN a busy law firm will tell you there's no such thing as a weekend. Sunday saw me hard at it, stuck in my office from seven am till well after six that evening. The criminal mastermind I'd been defending just before I met Evelyn, had decided to appeal his conviction. That left me scouring through trial documents and evidence lists searching for some sort of loop hole on which to base his appeal. I didn't like his chances. The prosecution had been thorough and their case appeared watertight. So sad. Too bad.

For almost a week, nothing had been heard of the woman I knew as Evelyn Rau. DI Dark and his team of intrepid law enforcers had turned the city upside down looking for her, but with no success. She'd simply vanished. On the upside, no other attacks similar to Mr Winster's murder had occurred, either in Brisbane, or for that matter anywhere else in the country since Monday night's attack. Popular conjecture was that she'd flown the coop. Probably in her private jet.

Working on the new appeal was taking its toll, but not as much as constantly worrying about what had happened to Evelyn. I hadn't had a decent night's sleep since the day she first walked into my life. I knew almost without question she was guilty of at least two murders, possibly more, but while my head told me she was a complete nutter and I was lucky to be rid of her, my heart still yearned for her touch. On the rare occasions that I did sleep, my dreams were full of images of her. One second she would be in my arms, telling me how much she loved me, the next she had me pinned down, wrapped tightly in a deadly embrace as she plunged a razor sharp knife into my throat. These dreams were so realistic I could swear I was awake. More worrying was that I was beginning to find even the most frightening and violent of them strangely alluring, almost erotic. Was I going insane?

I glanced at my watch and discovered it was almost seven. I saved the computer file I'd been working on and shut down the desktop. Fifteen minutes later I was behind the wheel of my old Ford, heading for home. I was beat. All I wanted to do was chuck a frozen pizza into the microwave, wash it down with a few light beers while I de-cluttered my brain in front of the idiot box. Then I'd climb into bed and sleep for a decade or so.

I wasn't going to get the chance.

Before I'd even put the key in the lock, I knew something was wrong. I could see a thin strip of light under the door and even though I'd left before dawn that morning, I knew I'd snapped off the light before heading for the office. I twisted the key and pushed open the door. Evelyn Rau, or whoever the hell she was, was sitting on my couch, facing the door as I entered. She was smiling. She was beautiful and she was dressed in a long, flowing, skin tight gown which once again showed off her voluptuous curves to perfection. The dress was split down the front to below her waist, revealing a narrow strip of perfect, creamy white, flesh. And yes, the dress was black.

I lunged towards the kitchen, threw open the cutlery drawer where I keep all my cooking knives and grabbed my biggest butchers knife.

"DON'T MOVE," I yelled. "I WON'T HESITATE TO USE THIS IF YOU DON'T KEEP PERFECTLY STILL."

I reached into my pocket for my cell phone, watching her closely as I did so. I knew she was dangerous, deadly dangerous, and I wasn't taking my eyes off her for a second. Carefully I dialled 000, the Australian emergency services number. But I never finished the call. Suddenly Evelyn sprang out of her seat like a cat, snatched the phone from my hand and quickly stepped away. She lifted the device to her ear. "Sorry," she said into it. " My child has been playing with my phone. Please disregard this call. There is no emergency. I am most sorry for disturbing you." Then she disconnected the call and turned the phone off. She stepped closer to me once more. Her hand shot out like a bolt of lightning and ripped the butcher's knife from my grasp. "You won't need this my Darling," she purred. "I would never hurt you my love. I only want for us to be together. Together for eternity. Just you and I. I love you Darling, surely you know that."

"What the hell's going on?" I demanded. "Who are you. Why did you kill those men?"

She smiled and ran the backs of her fingers gently over my cheek. "Oh Darling, you know why I had to kill them. You more than anyone else in the world know why they had to die. Their blood is the only thing which keeps me alive."

"BULLSHIT! What are you trying to tell me? That you're a vampire?

She smiled and rolled her eyes as if I was being obtuse.

"Vampires don't exist," I hissed at her. "They're just imaginary creatures, made up by some author with a vivid imagination to scare people. You need help Evelyn, or whoever the hell you are. You're delusional. You're not a vampire."

"Oh but I am, David," she told me. She smiled at me seductively. I felt she was just toying with me like some sort of cat playing with a mouse. "And your Great, Great Grandfather is partly responsible."

I lost my cool then. The whole conversation was ludicrous. "Abraham Van Helsing wasn't my Great Great Grandfather. The man never even existed. He's just a character in a book," I snapped.

"No he wasn't my darling. It appears your father has kept an important secret from you. Abraham van Helsing was your Great, Great Grandfather. He was as real as you and I."

She danced away from me, spinning around and around, smiling and laughing as if it was all just some terribly amusing joke.

"You know the story, David," she explained. "Everyone does: Lawyer Jonathan Harker travelled to Transylvania to assist Count Dracula with the purchase of a stately home in England. Dracula was the most powerful vampire in history. He enslaved the young man, feeding on his blood until he was close to death. Then he left him captive and at the mercy of his three blood sucking wives, while he travelled to England to take up residence in his recently acquired castle. Once in England Dracula met Harker's fiancée, Wilhelmina Murray and her young friend Lucy Westenra. Lucy became Dracula's next prey. He turned her into one of the undead. But your Great, Great Grandfather, Abraham van Helsing, drove a stake through her heart and saved her immortal soul. Then Dracula turned his attention to

Mina. Meanwhile, Jonathan Harker escaped the clutches of Dracula's brides and returned to England, where he married Mina. But he was too late. The Count had already begun to turn Jonathan's new wife into his next bride. Van Helsing, Jonathan Harker and the three men who had been vying for the love of Mina's friend Lucy, Dr Seward, Quincy Morris and Arthur Holmwood, chased Dracula back to his homeland and killed him. The story says that once The Count was killed, Mina Harker's soul was saved. She never completed the transition to Vampire."

"Yes, yes, I know all about the legend of Count Dracula and Abraham van Helsing. I've had that stupid story quoted to me my entire life. But it's make believe. Dracula is just a story. There was no such person as Abraham van Helsing, or Jonathan or Wilhelmina Harker. It's bullshit." I insisted.

Evelyn shook her head sadly. "You are wrong my love. Every word is true....Well not every word. The book's author, Bram Stoker, sanitized it a bit to make it more palatable for his readers. In fact, your Great, Great Grandfather didn't kill Dracula in time. Mina Harker's transformation into one of the undead was completed. But Jonathan's love for his new wife was so strong he refused to let van Helsing murder her, even though he knew it would release her soul from eternal damnation. Jonathan returned with her to England where he kept her prisoner, locked away from all others. He kept her alive by feeding her with the blood he drew from his own veins and from the veins of the poor, mad inmates from the near-by insane asylum, run by his friend Dr Seward. Once Jonathan past away, the task of caring for poor Mina fell upon Dr Seward. Now retired from running the asylum, he took Mina back to Transylvania, hoping to find a cure for what he considered to be some sort of supernatural infection. He believed that somewhere in Dracula's castle there existed some sort of historical document explaining how the Count became the terrifying creature he was, and hoped to find, in that document, a way to release the poor, tortured wife of his late friend. But Seward never found the solution. Mina Harker remained one of the undead.

One night Dr Seward became careless as he was feeding his charge. Mina attacked and killed him. Now she was free to take her sire's place as the ruler of Castle Dracula. For the next one hundred and twenty years she preyed upon the residents of the countryside around her castle. But eventually she was driven from her lair and was forced to seek refuge in another country."

"Oh, I get it. She came to Australia." I said derisively. "You're trying to tell me you're Mina Harker. Bullshit. You're just some delusional nutter who is responsible for the death of at least three people. You need to turn yourself in and get some serious help from a psychiatrist. You're fucking crazy."

I turned my back on her then and raced for the door, but she was too quick. She caught me by the arm and with strength which belied her delicate frame, spun me around to face her. Before I could stop her she grabbed me by the hair and pulled my face towards her. She kissed me, forcing my mouth open and pushing her tongue between my lips. My mouth filled with her blood. She'd bitten her own tongue, insanely believing the ridiculous myth that if a person drinks the blood of a vampire they too would become one of the undead. I pushed her away, spitting her vile plasma from my mouth. I felt sick. The bile rose up in my throat and I vomited onto the hallway carpet.

"It's too late my Darling," she told me, smiling. "Nothing can stop the process of conversion once it has begun. Now we will be together forever. We will live for all eternity, two creatures of the night, hunting together, feeding together. Together we will become more powerful than anyone can ever imagine. Two legends, Wilhelmina Harker and David van Helsing. Vampire and the Great, Great Grandson of the most famous Vampire slayer ever known, together as one."

She danced around the apartment, laughing and giggling like the mad woman she obviously was. "I came to kill you," she said, shaking

her head as if in amazement. "I wanted to kill the heir to the van
Helsing name. Your great, great grandfather could have saved me over
a century of torment. Instead he condemned me to to a living hell.
Harker and Seward barely kept me alive, kept me locked away while
they grew fat, living the high life. So I wanted to kill you, slowly,
painfully. I wanted to make you suffer. As I had suffered." She turned
towards me and I was amazed to see a tear well up in her eyes. "But then
I fell in love with you. For the first time in over a century I felt love in
my heart, David. We were meant to be together my love. And now we
shall be. Forever."

I lunged for the door, tore it open and raced out into the hallway.
I turned towards the elevator and ran smack bang into my personal
assistant Brenda. Her hair was pulled back in a tight blonde ponytail
and she was dressed in a long grey overcoat. Her face was set in a mask
of horror as she took in my blood soaked appearance.

"GET DOWN," she yelled as she threw open her coat and whipped
out a small but deadly looking speargun. I hit the deck just as she lifted
the weapon to her shoulder and squeezed the trigger. The aluminium
bolt hissed through the air as it flew over me, missing my head by mere
millimetres and I heard Evelyn scream as the projectile embedded itself
in her heart. I spun back around, just as the woman I loved dropped
to her knees, clutching the shaft of the multi barbed metal spear which
still protruded from her chest. She fell forward and lay twitching for a
few seconds in the throws of death, then lay still.

"Jesus David. Are you alright?" she asked, hurrying to my side. "I
thought that mad bitch was going to kill you. You're covered in blood.
She's the one who killed those two men down by the river, hey?"

I nodded, trying to catch my breath. Brenda put her arm under my
shoulder and helped me back inside my apartment. She sat me on the
couch and then went off to the kitchen, dampened a tea towel and then
returned to the living room and began to clean up my face and chest.

"Where did she stab you David? I can't see any puncture wound."

I took the towel from her and began to wipe the gunk off my chin. "I'm not hurt," I assured her. "It's not my blood. It's hers." Then I told her about Evelyn's attack.

"So she really thought she was a vampire? She believed she was this Mina Harker character from the novel 'Dracula'? What a nut case."

I nodded. " Yea, good thing you came along....What's the deal with the speargun?" I asked.

She shrugged. "Bought it from my neighbour. I'm going to take it with me on my holiday up to Airlie Beach. I brought it around for you to have a look at as I remembered you do a bit of spear fishing and I wanted to get your opinion before I handed over the cash."

"Well I don't know how good it'll be for catching fish, but it certainly works a treat on mad women."

I reached into my pocket for my phone to ring DI Dark. I needed to let him know I'd located Evelyn and that she'd been killed by my office assistant in self defence. Brenda went to my linen cupboard and retrieved an old blanket to cover my ex lover's corpse, we didn't want one of the neighbours stumbling across her dead body and having a heart attack. Seconds later she came hurtling back into the apartment.

"SHE'S GONE!" Brenda yelled. "THERE'S NO SIGN OF HER."

I hung up before I'd even finished dialling and joined Brenda in the hallway outside my front door. Sure enough there was no sign of Evelyn, not even a trace of blood on the carpet where she'd lain. She'd simply vanished. What the hell was going on?

WE NEVER FOUND OUT what happened to Evelyn's body. And without a corpse to prove she'd even been back to my home, Brenda and I decided to keep mum about her death. Too many unanswered; and unanswerable; questions to do anything else really. As far as DI Dark is concerned, she's still a fugitive. The cops never did discover her true identity. Also, how she got in and out of my apartment, through locked doors and without a key remains a mystery. I know what you're thinking. Maybe she really was a vampire. Well that's just ridiculous. Vampires don't exist. If they did, and Evelyn really was Mina Harker, I'd be a vampire now myself. I'm not, I promise, and you know how honest we lawyers are.

*But that was six months ago and although I still think of her often, the heartache is not so painful as it was. In time I'm sure I'll get over her completely. Thankfully, my legal practice is flourishing, and that keeps me busy and my mind occupied. So if you need a good legal council give me a call. My numbers in the book. Oh you'll need to phone after dark, I only work the night courts these days. Just can't seem to stay awake during the day anymore. How much do I charge? Well I won't be cheap, you know what we blood sucking lawyers are like.*

# Lost in the Outback

If there's one golden rule about breaking down in a remote area of Outback Australia, it's 'Stay with your Vehicle.' I know that. I've lived in what we Aussies call 'The Bush' my whole life. Only a complete Drongo walks away from his or her car or truck when they've had a prang. Only a fool wanders off into the bush when the shit hits the fan and they end up stuck kilometres from nowhere in a vehicle that won't go. So what's the rule? 'Stay with your vehicle!'

Why? Well a car or truck is much bigger than a human being and is therefore much easier to locate from the air. Also, unless you're driving something like an open topped Jeep, you've got some sort of roof over your head. Staying out of the sun in forty plus heat is essential to staying alive, and if you get desperate enough, at a pinch you may be able drink the water from the windscreen washer bottle. Plus if you need to attract the attention of the Emergency Services personnel looking for you, you can set fire to your spare tyre. That causes a huge, thick black pall of smoke which can be seen for miles.

How do you burn a tyre if you haven't got any matches to start a fire? Well you can get a spark by shorting out a pair of jumper leads attached to the vehicles battery. This can be used to ignite a small amount of fuel splashed over some dry sticks. I've even heard of someone starting a fire by dropping a wire wool pot scourer on the battery terminals, after they'd taken the battery out of the car of course. The dead short voltage heated the wire wool till it was red-hot in just a few seconds. They then used a stick to flick the glowing pot scourer onto some pages they'd torn from the car's owner's manual. Instant bonfire.

Oh! Just remember to let out all the air in the spare tyre before you set it alight, and of course, do it away from the car and in the middle of the road and somewhere where you're not going to start a bushfire.

But then, if you've been driving through remotest outback Australia, two hundred and thirteen kilometres from the nearest town, in a Jeep Cherokee, without a roof, with no water in the windscreen washer bottle and it rolled over and burst into flames, in the middle of the night when the flames and resulting thick black pall of smoke from all five burning tyres couldn't have been seen by anyone other than a mob of very frightened kangaroos, well then you're fucked.

That's exactly what's happened to me. So, I'm fucked.

I'd worked it all out. Three days ago I'd told my shithead business partner I was going hunting, though I didn't tell him what for. I informed the arsehole I would be back on Thursday, which is the day after tomorrow. Instead I doubled back and shot both him and his stupid brother in the back of the head as they sat, transfixed in front of the TV, watching their favourite midday soap opera. I'd discovered they were plotting to steal my money. I have six million dollars sitting in a term deposit which matures next March. It's been in the bank for the last five years. Only during one of those years have I been in partnership with Eric, so it's my money, not his. It's certainly not his fucking brother's.

My bank manager rang me a few days ago to let me know Eric had tried to withdraw the six mil' from the bank, claiming I'd authorized the withdrawal. He'd smelt a rat, told Eric it would take at least a week for the funds to be made available, and gave me a bell.

Eric's penchant for a flutter on the ponies is well-known throughout the small rural town where I run my business. My bank manager also knows that Eric's personal account is badly overdrawn and he's already knocked him back once, earlier in the year, when he asked for a personal loan.

So how did I end up with six million dollars in the bank? Five years ago I was a dirt poor sheep grazier. There's no money in wool anymore, synthetics are quicker and easier to produce, cost less and don't rely on good weather. Factories very rarely die of thirst during a drought. Of course wool's an infinitely superior fibre, so there is still a bit of a market for it. But it's nothing like what it was when my grandfather ran the station sixty years ago.

As a way to make a few extra bucks I'd done an on-line course in computer programming. I figured it didn't really matter where you lived when it came to the mystic art of coding. I was right. As long as a programmer has access to the www it doesn't matter a flying fuck where you live, you can still get lots of work. I've rented a small office in town where I get a modicum of internet access and have built up a small clique of clients.

One night a few years ago, it suddenly dawned on me, I could make a great deal of money if I could develop better software for the myriad of geological surveys the mining industry do around this part of our great and beautiful country. I won't bore you with the details, but the software I came up with, increases the likelihood of finding the valuable minerals mining companies look for by nearly seven percent. That might not sound like much, but trust me, such an increase is worth millions to the mining industry. World-wide, year to date, it's meant an increase in profitability for the companies who bought my software, by hundreds of millions. My share of the increased royalties has so far netted me a cool six million two hundred and sixty-one thousand, eight hundred and seventy-two dollars and counting.

Now I'm a man of simple tastes and requirements, plus there's not a lot of ways to spend such a windfall in the tiny town, currently two hundred and fifteen kilometres to my north-west, so most of it has ended up just earning a bit of interest in the bank.

So with all that money, how did the now lifeless hunk of shit formerly known as Eric come to be my business partner? Well the sheep don't shear themselves, plus they have to be drenched for parasites a couple of times a year. There's 'crutching' to stop them becoming fly blown. They have to be fed when the rain doesn't come and the grass doesn't grow, and a shit load of other things which have to be done on a sheep station. In years gone by, all of those things would have been done by me or one of my irregular employees. But of course now I have money, I'd rather get a dog than bark myself. I originally wanted to simply employ a manager, but Eric talked me into a partnership. It seemed like a good idea at the time. He wanted a share in the profits rather than a wage, and convinced me he knew exactly how the business should be run. We had the local legal beagle draw up a contract and both of us signed on the dotted line.

Bad move! I have to admit the guy knows everything there is to know about running a large sheep station, it's just he's proven on numerous occasions that I can't trust him as far as I can throw him. Considering I recently used the band-saw I butcher sheep for mutton when the shearing gang is in residence to cut him and his bother into chunks, none of which which wouldn't weigh any more than five kilograms, that's really saying something.

Of course I could have just given him his marching orders, but I'm still the major partner in our ill-conceived venture, and that would mean I would have had to buy him out. Fuck him. He'd bled enough out of me and my company over the past twelve months. It was time he did a bit of bleeding himself for a change.

Luckily his reputation is shit with just about everyone in the area. He owes money to at least a dozen people, so it won't be hard to convince everyone he and his brother have simply skipped town. My intention is to go to the cops and tell them Eric also stole a few thousand dollars from the safe in my office before he disappeared, thereby adding credence to my claim that he's a scumbag and I had nothing to do with the sudden disappearance of either him or his brother.

I got rid of the bodies down an old abandoned mine-shaft and circled back to town via a torturous route through the scrub, killing a few hours in the process and making sure I came back in from the opposite direction to the station.

All was going well until early this morning when the right front tire on the Jeep blew and I ended up upside down, in the middle of nowhere, in a burning vehicle. Miraculously, I managed to unclip my seatbelt and crawl away unharmed before the flames reached me.

It's now just a few minutes after dawn and I'm sitting on a big flat topped rock, staring down the dry and dusty dirt track that leads back, two hundred and thirteen kilometres, to the tiny hamlet where I have my office. I'm hoping like hell someone comes along soon so I can get out of here before the sun cooks me alive. Ironically, when I'm finally rescued, my predicament will actually work in my favour. I can tell the cops I crashed the car around midday yesterday. That means I couldn't have been anywhere near home when Eric and his stupid brother 'Robbed me and fucked off to unknown climes.' I'll be home and dry. No one will even suspect they're dead, never mind that I'm the dude who did the deed.

But no one's coming. It's already breathtakingly hot out here in the open. There's no shade to be found anywhere other than beside the burnt out wreck of my Jeep. I try to stand and find that my muscles won't work. It's like I'm glued to the fucking rock. As the sun inches its way into the sky, I try to raise my arm to cover my eyes and stop the insufferably bright glare from blinding me. I can't do it. I can't move. I'm paralysed.

But then, in the distance I can see the unmistakable sight of a cloud of dust thrown up by the tyres of a rapidly approaching vehicle. I pray for whoever it is to hurry. I can already feel the sun burning my skin. It's incredibly painful. Then I glance down at my body and scream. My skin is beginning to blister, smouldering waves of heat emanate from my chest and arms as if I'm being baked alive in an industrial furnace. I can see and feel my skin start to bubble and blacken, tiny flames sprout from my chest like wildflower blooms after a heavy downpour. Oh God! I'm on fire.

Through unbearable pain and terror, unable to move a muscle, I watch helplessly as an old Toyota Land Cruiser skids to a halt beside the wreckage of my vehicle. I cry out to the Toyota's occupants. A wizened old bloke I vaguely recognize from a Rotary meeting earlier in the year and his wife, gets out of the vehicle, but he doesn't seem to hear me. His spindly form shuffles over to the wreck, his equally ancient and skeletal wife joining him a few seconds later.

"Shit!" the old man exclaims. "Hell of a crash. Don't see how anyone could have walked away from that." He stoops over, grunting from his arthritis and unaccustomed exertion as he does so, and peers under the car. "There's no driver," he tells his wife. "Perhaps he was thrown clear."

"I'M OVER HERE!" I scream. "PLEASE HELP ME. But once again they ignore me. As I cry and yell for help, they wander around aimlessly, searching the area around the Jeep as if they were looking for something.

Perhaps I was going insane. Perhaps I'd been knocked unconscious in the crash and this was all just a terrible nightmare. But how in hell could I be in so much pain and not wake up?

Suddenly the old man and his wife are beside me, looking down at me as if in horror.

The ancient old crone swears, repeating her husband's curse of a few minutes earlier. "Shit. Is that who I think it is?"

"I think so," her husband replies. "Hard to tell, him all being smashed up and burnt to a crisp like that. I guess he must have been consumed by the fire but still managed to crawl away from the Jeep somehow. We'd better go back to Brian's place and use his phone to call the cops."

"Poor man," the woman said, looking down at my inert body with tears in her eyes. "He must have suffered terribly before he died." Then they turned around and slowly walked back to their Land Cruiser.

I see and hear their car thunder past me now at least once a month on their way to see Brian. Who Brian is I have no way of knowing. I assume he's either their son or perhaps just a neighbour.

The cops came and towed away my car. Then later another couple of the boys in blue turned up in a Nissan Patrol Paddy Wagon. I saw them open up the back, drag out a stretcher and retrieve what I have come to realize must have been my mortal remains. As they lifted my body into the back of the van I could see it was little more than a charred and misshapen lump of flesh. How the hell I had managed to crawl away from the wreck like that, is a mystery.

They've gone now, leaving me to suffer alone for the rest of eternity. The hours pass slowly out here. Each and every second of daylight is spent reliving the agony of the fire which took away my life. Once the sun goes down the agony stops. I'm granted a few short hours of relief. My screams of pain cease to echo silently across the arid emptiness of the vast Australian desert. But my night-time succour is fleeting. I know with unswerving certainty that the torture will begin again in a few short hours. Every second of darkness brings me closer to that certainty that the sun will always rise. Every passing moment is filled with terror of what I know must surely come.

Each day as the sun peaks its fiery head over the horizon my soul begins to burn once more and I am once again propelled into an ocean of unbelievable agony.

I know what has happened now. I have been condemned to the fires of hell for the murder of my former business partner Eric and his brother. I realize now that hell really exists.

It's in the middle of nowhere, two hundred and thirteen kilometres from the nearest town, somewhere in Outback Australia.

At least my hell is.

# The Trap.

*(Translated from Formosan Chinese into English with the invaluable assistance of Mr Michael Chow.)*

My name is Wai Fong. I am twenty years old. My uncle is one of the diplomats at the Taiwanese Embassy in Canberra. He's not the Ambassador you understand, just one of the diplomatic staff who live and work in the Embassy. He was kind enough to arrange a visa and a plane ticket for me so I could come to Australia and visit him. I wish he hadn't. If I'd stayed at home, I wouldn't be in the huge amount of shit I'm in now.

"You're my favourite niece," my uncle told me on the phone. "I'd love for you to come and see this beautiful country. Tell my brother there will be a plane ticket waiting for you at the airport. I'll see you in eighteen days."

I could hardly wait. Ever since my uncle was posted to 'The Land Down Under', I had been dreaming of visiting that wonderfully interesting country. My uncle had spoken to my Dad on numerous occasions, always waxing lyrically about what a great country it was. It sounded like the perfect place for a young, university educated woman to take a holiday.

In high school I had learnt to speak English. All Taiwanese high school students do these days. I was far from proficient, but I knew I'd mastered it well enough to get by. Provided of course, people spoke slowly and gave me time to translate the words in my head. Reading and writing were a different matter. No matter how hard I studied, I just couldn't get my head around the totally weird symbols the Australians used in their writing. I have however, managed to memorize the way certain words look. I can for example, recognize the words for toilet-Ladies and Gents- the words Hostel and Airport. I can of course, also identify words like McDonald's and Pizza and Lager, so I knew I wasn't going to starve. Besides, many of my friends had travelled overseas, and they all told me the best thing to do was to pair up with someone who speaks English as a first language. People from Australia and England of course were always a good choice. New Zealanders, Americans and most Canadians too. Many Germans speak English well. Almost all Dutch speak and read English fluently, as do a great many French. Plus most kids doing the 'Backpacker' thing prefer to travel with a partner or in a group anyway.

I spent almost a month with my uncle and aunt in Canberra and then shrugged my backpack onto my back and caught a greyhound to Sydney. My uncle had explained that the bus would take me to the city and stop at a big, bus depot. There I would find any number of smaller buses, run by the multitude of Backpacker Hostels in Sydney, who would take me to their hostel for free if I stayed at their hostel for at least one night. He felt my plan of hooking up with another girl and travelling together was a good one. It didn't quite work out that way.

My first night in Sydney was spent at the 'Harbour View Hostel'. Although I didn't see even a hint of that city's world-famous harbour. The place was both clean and tidy as well as comfortable. I was lucky, or maybe I should say unlucky, enough to meet a Dutch girl, just four months older than me, who was planning to head up the east coast of Australia in two days time. We decided to travel together.

The Dutch girls name was Vodi. She was tall and blonde, with big, round, blue eyes, pale skin and a happy smile. Unfortunately she was also a thieving bitch. Our friendship lasted only six days. By that time we hated each other. In my case at least, I felt I had good reason. Vodi stole almost all my money and spent it on drugs, and though I didn't realize until later, she'd also stolen my bus ticket. We went our separate ways on the morning of the seventeenth. Vodi left on the Greyhound at nine am, leaving me stranded in a tiny outback town called Galstone. It was there my nightmare began.

Vodi and I had been travelling by Greyhound Bus, stopping at various places which caught our interest and then moving on when we'd seen whatever there was to see. I couldn't afford to buy another bus ticket, so I decided to try my hand (thumb?) at hitch-hiking. Stupid, stupid girl.

I'd met a large number of other travellers since arriving in Oz. Many of them had tried hitch-hiking at some point during their travels. It was simply the cheapest way to see the country. There were, however, a few impediments to my embracing that mode of transport wholeheartedly.

One: I was by myself which made it potentially dangerous. (I'd seen 'Wolf Creek') Two: my English wasn't very good. Three: Although lots of people do it, hitch-hiking is actually illegal in Australia. And four: According to the news programs I'd seen on TV over the past few nights, four young women had been attacked in the area over the last three months. They had all been raped and brutally murdered.

But, on the pro hitch-hiking front there were a number of factors in its favour. One: Only one bus came through Galstone each day and I'd already waved goodbye to it with my middle finger earlier that morning. Two: Thanks to the light-fingered Dutch fiend, until I could get my Dad to wire me some more money, I couldn't afford a bus ticket anyway. Three: Australia is a very expensive country for a twenty-year-old Taiwanese University student travelling around on a shoestring budget, even if I hadn't been robbed. Hitch-hiking was free. Four: Well, there wasn't a number four. I just didn't have any other choice.

Stupid, stupid, extremely stupid girl!

I heaved my backpack onto my shoulders, walked to the highway, smiled sweetly and stuck out my thumb. The first vehicle that came along, less than five minutes later, was an old and extremely dirty Toyota Land Cruiser. It pulled over. The driver looked questioningly at me and then reached over and opened the passenger door. He smiled, grunted and waved me onboard. I threw my backpack on the back seat and climbed in.

"Thank you for your kindness Sir," I said in my best English. "I wish to travel with you to the north. I am heading for Balina".

He grunted at me again, threw the car into gear and accelerated quickly, the vehicle's tyres squealing loudly on the road surface and filling the interior with the car with the smell of burning rubber.

I looked over at my new chauffeur. He was an older man, perhaps a year or two older than my father. He had long, grey, greasy hair, which he had tied back in a ponytail. His face was deeply scored and tanned by the blistering Australian sun, and his eyes were as blue as the deepest ocean. My mother would have called him handsome in a rough, unkempt sort of way. I wasn't so sure. He was dressed in a faded brown, check shirt, ancient dark blue jeans and a pair of scuffed and worn, heavy duty work boots.

"My name is Wai Fong," I told him. He ignored me.

"What is your name Sir?" I enquired. Again he ignored me. I began to feel decidedly uneasy.

"Are you going to Balina?' I asked. No response. I began to panic. Why didn't he speak?

He glanced my way and smiled. He pointed to his ear and shook his head indicating he couldn't hear me.

"Oh!" He was hard of hearing. I twisted around in my seat, reached over and rummaged through my backpack. I got out my well thumbed road map of the east coast of New South Wales. I tapped him on the shoulder to get his attention and pointed to the map, indicated the town of Balina, just a few centimetres south of the border with

Queensland and the start of the world-famous 'Gold Coast'. Sun drenched beaches, bronzed surfer guys, twenty-four hour nightlife. All the things a young woman could want or need for a perfect beachside holiday. "BALINA", I said loudly. He snorted with derision and waved his hands in the air. It looked like he was using sign language. Oh! He was deaf, not just hard of hearing.

Keeping one eye on the road he pointed a grubby finger at my map indicating the town of Galstone, then traced his finger along the road until it reached Coffs Harbour. He stabbed at the page a couple of times and then at himself to clarify his meaning. Then he skipped back to Galstone and once again traced the road to Coffs Harbour. He reached into his shirt pocket and pulled out a pen. He wrote '200 k' on my map and once more traced his finger from Galstone to Coffs harbour.

Then he continued on to Balina. '300 K' he wrote. I understood his meaning. He was only going as far as Coffs harbour. Balina was another three hundred kilometres further north. I nodded my thanks. I keep forgetting just how big Australia is.

We drove on in silence for about half an hour. Suddenly my new friend tapped me on the shoulder and pointed out the window towards the side of the road. There were cows grazing on the verge. Big deal. I'd seen cows before. We even have them in Taiwan. I turned and smiled at him, nodding my head to tell him I'd seen them. He grunted at me again and once more pointed urgently at the roadside. Perhaps there was something else he was wanting me to see. I turned my head and peered out the window, trying to gauge exactly what it was the man was trying to show me. I heard him rattling around for something in the side pocket of his door and then I felt a sharp pain in my thigh. I looked down to find a hypodermic syringe sticking out of my leg.

The last thing I saw before the world turned black and I passed out, was the deaf man grinning at me as if he'd just won the lottery. Shit. Looks like I'm going to be victim number five.

I WOKE UP LYING INSIDE a tent. I knew it was a tent because it
was made of bright orange, waterproof polyester, it was shaped like a
tent, and I was lying on top of a sleeping bag. Plus I recognized it. It was
my tent. The contents of my backpack were piled neatly on the floor
next to me, but my hiking boots and socks were missing. My feet were
bare. My head was pounding and I was having difficulty focusing.

The front of the tent was open, allowing me to see out. I was
greeted by the breathtaking vista of a beautiful, blue lake just a dozen
metres from my 'doorstep'. Between the tent and the lake was a small
campfire, and next to the campfire, the deaf man was hunched over,
stirring something in a large, smoke blackened pot. Whatever he was
cooking smelt delicious.

Gingerly I raised myself up on one elbow and edged closer to the
opening, searching for an avenue of escape. My head swum and a wave
of nausea washed over me. I collapsed back onto the sleeping bag and
once again passed out, though this time only for a few moments. When
I awoke once more, I found the man had dragged me outside. He'd
propped me up against the trunk of a big iron bark tree and placed
a plastic plate laden with some sort of stew near my right hand. The
plastic spoon sticking out of the middle of the dish didn't look like a
very practical weapon to defend myself with.

My abductor was sitting cross-legged a couple of metres to my left.
He was shovelling food into his mouth with a fork. He looked angry
and determined.

He pointed to my brimming plate with his fork and mimed eating.
Clearly he wanted me to eat the stew he had prepared. I was terrified.
What the hell was going on? I started to cry.

As he couldn't speak, I surmised he had been deaf since birth. If
that was the case then it was likely he could read lips. I crawled closer
to him, looked him directly in the eye and begged him not to hurt me.

But all he did was once again point to his ear and shake his head. He watched my lips closely however, so I was pretty sure he knew what I was saying. He also looked extremely uncomfortable.

I struggled to my feet and tried to run. I was still dizzy and the ground around the tent was uneven and strewn with large rocks. I had only taken a few steps before I fell heavily. I quickly struggled to my feet once more and ran on. The hard ground was murder on my unshod feet. Within seconds they began to hurt like I was running over broken bottles. I blotted out the pain as best I could and continued to limp painfully towards the safety of the trees. I glanced behind me. My abductor hadn't moved. He was still sitting there, slowly eating his stew, watching me hobble painfully over the stony ground. I reached the tree line and searched for some sort of trail which might lead me back to the highway. I had no idea where I was, but hurried on regardless as quickly as I could, stumbling through the dense forest. Anywhere was better than staying with a silent murderer.

Then suddenly he was standing in front of me, shaking his head as if I were some disobedient puppy who had soiled the carpet. He grabbed me by the shoulders, spun me around, back towards the campsite and pushed me forward. With no other choice I took a few steps and then collapsed to the ground. My feet were a bloody mess. They were cut to shreds.

The man reached down, wrapped one arm around my waist and lifted me over his shoulder as if I were as light as a feather. A few minutes later he dumped me back on the ground outside my tent. He picked up my dish of stew and shoved it in my hands. Then he placed his hand on top of my head and pressed down firmly. His meaning was clear. I was to stay there. I wasn't to move. My tears cascaded down my face once more. I was trapped. The deaf man was going to kill me and no one would ever find my body.

MY KIDNAPPER MADE COFFEE. Hot sweet and milky. He handed me a plastic cup, filled to the brim and then went back to where he'd been sitting and retrieved a few sheets of writing paper. He handed them to me, then turned and walked away. I watched in total confusion as he disappeared into the forest.

I looked at the pages he had given me. On them were lines and lines of writing, all of which meant nothing to me. I recognized a few of the words, but the meaning of what he had written was unfathomable. I still had no idea what the hell was going on. Was he going to come back? Was this how he killed his victims, left them stranded in the middle of the Australian bush and waited for them to starve to death?

On hands and knees I searched the area around the camp ground. There, on the other side of the campfire was a large wooden box. Inside was lots of tinned food. Meat, vegetables, potatoes, tinned fruit, plus cans of dried milk. There was a large box of breakfast cereal, tea and coffee, chocolate and other confectioneries, plus a whole gamut of other edible stuff including a dozen large bottles of water. Enough food in fact, for a whole week for two people. There were matches to relight the fire if it went out, and plenty of firewood chopped ready next to the box. Oh well, I thought, at least he doesn't want me to starve.

I crawled over to the tent and hunted through my belongings for something to use as a weapon. There was nothing more dangerous than my tooth brush. I had similar success trying to find footwear. The bastard had taken my boots plus my only other pair of shoes. He hadn't even left me with a pair of socks. I grabbed my old towel and a tracksuit top and wrapped them around my feet, tying them in place with the cord from my tracksuit pants and the belt from my good sundress. Then I hobbled down to the lake's edge and soaked my aching feet in the chilly water. I washed away the dirt and blood and inspected the damage. I had a big, but thankfully shallow cut on my left heel and my right big toe was severely lacerated. There were also numerous tiny nicks and cuts all over the soles of my feet, but nothing major. All in all

I concluded, they felt much worse than they were. They hurt like hell. I rewrapped my feet and using a stout stick as a crutch, made my way back to the tent. My abductor was still nowhere to be seen.

To the east of my campsite was a small, boulder strewn hill. It was, perhaps, fifty metres high and at most a kilometre from my present position. Hopefully I would be able to see the highway from the top. I took off for the hill as fast as my aching feet would allow.

It took me over an hour of hobbling to reach the hill and climb to the top. I looked around. Everywhere I looked there was nothing but trees. Dense forest extended away in all directions, all the way to the horizon. I knew the coast must be somewhere over to the east, and in all probability, the highway was somewhere between where I was standing and the ocean. But how far? I had no idea how long had I been unconscious? I could be hundreds of kilometres inland. To try to walk out, with no shoes and only a very vague idea of where I was going would be madness. I slumped down on the ground and wept once more. I was trapped. I wasn't going anywhere and the monster who had kidnapped me knew it.

I BARELY SLEPT THAT night. I kept the fire going the whole time, building it up by dragging fallen branches and sticks over to it and throwing them on until I had a raging inferno. I figured the flames might be seen by a passing car or aircraft and at the same time keep away any dangerous animals. My kidnapper still hadn't returned by dark, so I guessed he wouldn't be back before morning. I crawled into my tent, coming back out again every time I felt the fire needed more fuel. It was a long night.

The man didn't return the next day either. I ate breakfast. Hobbled about the campsite collecting firewood. Washed myself in the lake. Made lunch. Began writing this journal and then, late in the afternoon, I had a nap. I was so exhausted I started to see dark spots before my eyes and developed a raging head ache. I slept fitfully though, always keeping one eye open, just in case the monster who had abducted me suddenly returned. He didn't. Later, as the sun sank slowly in the west, I opened a tin of of beans, heated them over the fire and sat cross-legged on the edge of the lake, shovelling them into my mouth with my plastic spoon. I gasped, there on the other side of the lake was a mob of kangaroos. There was about a dozen animals. They'd come down to the water's edge to drink. They were the first kangaroos I'd seen since coming to Australia. They were a beautiful pale brown colour with darker brown stripes along their cheeks. The stood up tall, watching me from the opposite bank and then, realizing I wasn't a threat, dropped their heads and resumed drinking.

I became angry then. My campsite was in a beautiful place, filled with wonderful and interesting wild life. I'd seen Kangaroos, Kookaburras, the big lizards the Aussies called a Goanna and all manner of birdlife. I'd even seen an Emu. To camp at such a glorious, secluded spot should have been a wonderful experience. Instead I was terrified, lost and alone and fearing for my life. I'd been drugged, kidnapped, injured and subjected to utter terror by a rapist and a murderer, and all because I'd been foolish enough to befriend a thief who'd stolen all my money, forcing me to hitch-hike.

The second night of my ordeal was entirely different to the first. Early in the evening the clouds rolled in from the west. They were thick and black and swirled viscously, like an inverted cauldron of boiling oil. Lightning flashed with fearsome intensity in the distance and thunder boomed across the sky. Around 8:00 pm the heavens opened and the rain came down in huge silver sheets. I'd never seen such a heavy downpour. The sound of the rain drumming on the roof of my little tent was almost deafening. It continued to bucket down until around midnight when the rain finally began to ease.

When I awoke the next morning, the sun was once again blazing brilliantly in the sky and there was little sign of the deluge of the previous night. The ground and the trees around my campsite were wet of course, but there was no sign of flooding and none of my essential food or equipment had washed away.

But the fire had been well and truly swamped.

At first I wasn't too concerned about the fire. I would eat cold cereal for breakfast and there was fresh fruit for lunch, plus I could manage without a hot meal at night. But, there was that all important need to attract attention. If I was going to make it back to civilization alive, I needed to keep my signal fire burning. I wasted half a box of matches trying to get the damp kindling to light before I finally realized I was fighting a losing battle. I needed something dry, something which would burn easily until the kindling dried out. I could use the pages from my diary, but I wanted to keep the record of my abduction intact. If I died, my parents and the people who loved me would need to know what had happened. This meant I had to keep the journal whole and had to leave it where someone would find it.

My other option was to use the pages my abductor had left with me. No doubt the words he'd written there were important to him. But I couldn't read them anyway. They were in English. I laid the damp kindling in the sun to dry and then, late in the afternoon, I put a match to the pages and carefully fed the resulting flame with small bits of wood, gradually placing each piece on top, so I didn't smother the flame. Soon I had a raging fire blazing once more.

As I'd hoped my signal fire finally attracted someone's attention. Unfortunately it attracted the wrong person.

It was just two hours before dusk when a slightly built man with a rucksack on his back walked into the clearing. He was around fifty years of age, with scrawny arms and legs, a prominent nose and a weak chin. His thinning hair was plastered to his head with sweat and his clothes were rank with filth. There was a bright red scar slashed across his forehead, He took one look at me, threw down his rucksack and began to chuckle insidiously. Suddenly he rushed towards me, screaming

obscenities. He grabbed me and threw me to the ground. He jumped
on top of me. Pining me down as he tried to tear the clothes from my
body. He grabbed my left breast and squeezed it painfully, making me
cry out in pain. It was then I realized that this man, not my abductor,
was the person responsible for the rape and murder of the four young
girls I'd heard about. He was about to make me number five.

My attacker raised himself up on one elbow as he tried to extricate
himself from his pants. He looked down at me and leered. There was
a sickening thud, like someone had hit a watermelon with a baseball
bat and the evil little man was thrown sideways. Standing there in the
gathering twilight was my abductor. In his hand he carried a blood
soaked axe. The rapist was surely dead, and yet the deaf guy dragged
him off me and in a frenzy of unbelievable violence struck his victim
again and again with his axe until the man's head was nothing but a
bloody pulp. Then he grabbed him by the ankle and dragged him off
into the forest.

I should have jumped to my feet and quickly run as far away from
that horrific carnage as possible. But I was frozen by the trauma of the
rapist's attack. I was unable to move.

Moments later the deaf man returned from disposing of his victim's
body. He picked up his axe and hurled it as far as he could into the lake,
then staggered down to the water's edge and dove in, fully clothed. He
quickly began to wash the blood and gore from his body. After a few
minutes he clambered out again, strode purposefully to my tent and
crawled inside. He came out seconds later with a pair of my jeans and a
t-shirt. He handed them to me and pointed to the lake. I realized that I
too was splattered with gore.

As I sat on the gravel at the waters edge washing my attackers blood
and brains from my body, the deaf man hurried around the campsite,
packing away all my possessions and stuffing them in my backpack. He
quickly disassembled my tent, rolled it up tightly and strapped it to the
rucksack. Then he went over to the food box and dragged it to one side.

Underneath, hidden in a shallow hole in the ground, were my hiking boots and socks. When I'd finished washing and had dressed in clean clothes, he handed them to me and waited while I put them on. Then he heaved my backpack onto his shoulders, gently took my hand and led me into the forest.

It took only ten minutes or so of trekking through the trees before we reached his old Toyota Land Cruiser. He'd hidden it from view under a canopy of fallen branches. To the casual observer it was virtually invisible. He dragged away the branches, opened the passenger side door and beckoned me in. Then he went around to his side, clambered in and started the ancient vehicles diesel. Half an hour later we were back at the highway. He stopped at the intersection and turned right, back towards Galstone.

Suddenly he pulled over, stopped the car by the side of the road and turned off the motor. He sat there silently for several long moments. Then his head sank forward slowly until his forehead rested on the steering wheel. He let out a low cry like a wounded animal and began to cry. The tears poured from his eyes, dripping wetly onto the legs of his jeans, once again soaking the fabric.

Half an hour later we stopped again, this time just outside a tiny graveyard on the outskirts of Galstone. He climbed out of the car, walked around to my side and opened the door. Gently he took my had and led me through the cemetery, to a grave over near the back fence. The words on the headstone read:

# Elizabeth Mccullough.
# 1<sup>St</sup> November 2001 — 3<sup>rd</sup> March 2017

And then some other words I couldn't understand. The deaf man reached into his back pocket and pulled out his wallet. He opened it and showed me a photo of himself and a dark haired, slim woman about the same age. They were standing either side of a young girl with their arms wrapped around her. There was a birthday cake with the number 16 written on it in blue icing. She was just sixteen years old.

I looked up at Mr McCullough. Once again there were tears in his eyes. I faced him so he could see my lips.

"He murdered your daughter?" I asked, pointing back down the highway towards the camp ground with one hand, and drawing my finger across my forehead, were the rapists scar had been with the other, so it was perfectly clear to Elizabeth's father who I was talking about.

He nodded sadly. I'd finally guessed what the past three days had been all about. The rapist and murderer had been in the area before. Elizabeth McCullough had been a victim of some earlier killing spree. Of course, I now wished I hadn't burnt the letter he had written for me. No doubt those pages would have explained what he was planning and would have answered some of the unanswered questions I still had; like how exactly he had lured his daughter's killer to the secluded campsite?

In fact, all I knew for certain, was that the whole thing had never been about me.

I'd just been the bait.

We reached Galstone just as the last rays of the dying sun dipped down behind the hills to the west of the tiny town. Mr McCullough drove down Main Street, did a U-turn and parked the old Land Cruiser outside a modern looking, red brick building. The place was lit up brightly, and through the large sliding glass doors at the front of the building, I could see a man in uniform working diligently behind a chest high counter. On the front of the building was an oval, blue and white, neon sign. On it was another word I recognized. POLICE. Mr McCullough reached across and pushed open my door. He nodded, letting me know it was okay for me to get out, then he unclipped his seatbelt and started to open his own door. It seemed he was going to turn himself in.

He was right to do that of course. He'd taken the law into his own hands. He'd killed the man who had murdered his daughter. Plus he'd abducted me, drugged me, left me stranded, terrified and alone in the middle of nowhere. Now it seemed, although he'd set out to extract a terrible vengeance on the man who'd slain his daughter, he'd fully understood there would be a price to be paid after he'd done so. He understood that society would want their pound of flesh.

But hadn't the man sitting next to me already suffered enough? I can't even begin to comprehend the utter, soul-destroying grief felt by parents who have lost a child. How much more devastating must it have been for Elizabeth's father, knowing that his daughter, his child, his baby, had been murdered by an insane sex fiend?

The man who had attacked me deserved to die. Of that I was certain. I was now also sure that I had never been in any real danger. I'm convinced Mr McCullough was watching over me the whole time, just waiting for that insane bastard to show up so he could kill him.

My damaged feet would heal quickly. Not so the broken heart of my new friend. Surely that was more than a pound of flesh. It was for me. Society could go to hell.

As he turned to climb out of the car, I reached over and gently touched his shoulder. He turned back to me and I shook my head, telling him no, don't do this. I rummaged through my backpack and pulled out my well-worn map of the east coast of New South Wales. I pointed at our current location, the tiny town of Galstone, then traced my finger northwards, along the highway, two hundred kilometres, to the city of Coffs harbour. The place where, three days ago, he'd told me he lived. I tapped the spot emphatically. I made sure he could see my lips.

"Take me there." I said. "That's were we should go."

He nodded sadly, then started the car. We said goodbye to each other three hours later.

### The End

# Don't miss out!

Visit the website below and you can sign up to receive emails whenever Kevin William Barry publishes a new book. There's no charge and no obligation.

https://books2read.com/r/B-A-JODC-RXYT

**BOOKS 2 READ**

Connecting independent readers to independent writers.

Did you love *Murder, Mayhem and Mystery. A Collection of Short Stories*? Then you should read *A Pain In The Arts*[1] by Kevin William Barry!

*Sally Croft and her unborn son are brutally murdered. The cops have arrested someone, but Sally's husband Daniel is convinced they've got the wrong person.*

*He tracks the man he thinks is responsible to Far North Queensland, Australia and sets about collecting evidence. But is Daniel seeking justice or just revenge, and what is the secret behind the painting "Miesbach Castle"? a secret so powerful it will cause a seemingly harmless man to commit Murder.*

---

# Also by Kevin William Barry

**The Flying Tiger Series**
Charlotte and the Morthe
Charlotte and the Creatures of Habit

**Standalone**
A Murderous Addiction
Innocent Until Proven Deadly
Dead Tropical
A Lethal Odyssey
A Pain In The Arts
Alien Vermin
Murder In The Outback
Murder, Mayhem and Mystery. A Collection of Short Stories
The Rich and The Dead
Fart From the Madding Crowd
The Voyage
Assassination Shuffle

# About the Author

Kevin William Barry is the Australian author of numerous novels.

He lives on the Atherton Tableands, Far North Queensland Australia with his wife Cathy